A Thug's Promise
By: Quisha Dynae

Chapter 1

Reeno

The coppery smell that lingered in the air around me caused me to cringe. I would never let anyone know it bothered me though. Someone may get it twisted and think that I was weak. The high-pitched scream exiting my victim's mouth pierced everyone's ears just as I connected my fist to Nelly's face.

The lighting in this bitch was dim, and there was water dripping from spots in the ceiling. I was just ready to get out of here. I wiped sweat from above my brow as I peered at the half-dead muthafucka who thought that is was OK to steal from me and my brother, Raydon.

This was the part of my job that I didn't like. Taking a life never got easier, but hey, sometimes it needed to be done. Especially when a nigga thought that he could just steal from you and thought you weren't smart enough to figure the shit out. A nigga like me had all the common sense and street smarts in the world, so it's beyond me why a nigga would try me like that, especially one of my top soldiers that had been by my side since day one. It's not much that can get past me. The fact that it only took me a day to figure out someone was stealing my product and money, and just a week to figure out who it was lets you know I'm not a dumb nigga. To say I was disappointed was an understatement. This nigga had me questioning my damn self.

"I trusted you, my nigga. What were you thinking? I would have given you the clothes off my back, Nelly. You know how I operate, nigga!" I yelled, seething just looking at this nigga who was supposed to be my homie.

"Come on, Reeno, man. Please don't do this. I'm sorry." Nelly was begging for his life. I would have had more respect for him if he took his punishment like a man instead of begging like a bitch. I was the boss, and there was no room in my camp for a snake. I lifted the chain that was wrapped around my hand and came down on Nelly's left thigh.

"Ahhhhhhhhh!" he screamed as his leg opened up to the white meat. Blood squirted out, getting on my brand-new Timberland boots, further pissing me off. I swung the chain again, but this time, on his other thigh, followed by his shoulder.

"Damn, nigga. Is all that necessary? Just shoot the nigga," my brother, Raydon, expressed like this shit really bothered him. It was he and I, along with Zack and Chad. They were my white boys, responsible for all cleanups. They were already getting dressed in their disposable jumpsuits, anxious to complete their job. I paid them well, so it was nothing that they wouldn't do for me. Nelly was moaning at this point. He could hardly keep his head up from the pain that he was enduring.

"Just kill me, man. I can't take it, Reeno. I'm sorry, man. Please forgive me."

"Man, put this nigga out his misery, bruh. This shit nasty." Raydon frowned at me.

"Don't rush me, nigga. Do I rush you when you handling your business?"

I grabbed a bottle of rubbing alcohol off of the table next to me and opened the top before looking to my brother for an answer. Raydon only looked at me, shaking his head.

"Exactly, nigga." I doused Nelly's wounds with the bottle of rubbing alcohol, causing him to wake up because he had passed out. I then grabbed the matches that were also on the table and asked Nelly,

"You ready to meet the devil?" Nelly's eyes stretched wide once he saw what was in my hand.

"No, no, no, no, no. Ahhhhhhhhhh!" Nelly screamed as I lit the match and threw it onto his wound on his right thigh, and then I lit another one, throwing it on his shoulder. The rancid smell of burning flesh immediately filled the air as Nelly squirmed in the chair he was tied to, causing it to fall over onto the floor with a loud thud. I was finished. I knew he would be dead soon.

"A'ight, y'all." I turned to Zack and Chad before continuing to say,

"Do what y'all do." I pulled out an envelope containing $60,000 in it, handing it to Zach.

"We appreciate it, man. There will not be one trace when we're done," Chad let me know. I extended my hand to shake both of theirs before I left our torture chambers with my brother following close behind. When we made our way upstairs, I let out a sigh before walking into my office. I sat down, looking down at my boots, knowing I had to change them so that no one would be looking at me funny. I slipped them off of my feet, throwing them to the side as I grabbed my gym bag to change clothes altogether.

"Man, bruh, I really can't believe Nelly ended up being a snake. I remember when he used to hang with us heavy, then all of a sudden he changed," my brother, Raydon, commented.

"Yeah, I know. But check it, that nigga gone, so there is no reason to bring his whack ass up," I explained to Raydon as I pulled a t-shirt over my head.

"I feel you. You trying to go to Pops' place?" my brother asked, speaking of our father, Stanford's, Cigar/strip Bar.

"Yeah, we can do that," I let him know before grabbing my keys and walking out of the door. My brother hopped in his G-Wagon, and I jumped in mine as we followed each other twenty minutes away to Pop's lounge. Stepping out of the car, I walked up to the door, dapping up Deuce, my pops' bodyguard. This nigga was big, black, and ugly. If I wasn't who I was, I would be scared of that nigga.

Raydon

I pulled up to my crib; you know it must be some secluded type shit, hidden by tall mothafuckin' trees. Laying my head where others would have a hard time finding was a must for the boy. Couldn't just have mothafuckas being able to just ride by and see me walking out my house. Nah, my shit was so ducked off I could walk outside naked and a bitch couldn't see. Shit, I didn't even have mail coming to this shit.

This weed had me so relaxed that I didn't even realize I was just sitting in the car. I was home and still sitting in the damn car. As I turned the car off, all I could do was think about sliding into something warm and wet and bust this nut. I needed to wind down from today's event, and a nut was the best reliever.

People thought that running an empire was easy work. They thought that all you did was delegate mothafuckas, but that's the furthest from the truth. Like tonight, it was hard as fuck to lay a nigga's life down that I knew for years. But I couldn't let that shit go, because then others would have thought it was OK to steal from us. Weakness couldn't be afforded, no matter who the fuck it was.

"It's about time," Destiny spoke the minute I closed the front door behind me, making me grab my dick through my pants. She stood on the left side of the double staircase with one hand planted on the gold rail. She had on some sexy ass yellow lingerie that clung to her curves like a too small condom clinging on to my dick.

I fucked with Destiny the long way. We weren't official or no shit like that, but I kept her around 'cause she had some good pussy. She was the closest thing to a girlfriend that I'd ever had. I imagined when I was ready to settle down, she would be the one I'd settle down with.

Destiny wasn't only good pussy, but she had a good head on her shoulders. She was older than me by four years, making her twenty-seven. Baby had her own shit and didn't stress me out about spending my money on her.

"What's good, baby?" I slipped my arm around her waist and kissed her long, silky neck.

I let go of her and then said, "Let me go shower real quick." I then walked toward my massive bathroom.

Once I washed the remnants of the day off of my body, I walked out of the bathroom butt ass naked, ready to get it in. I only dried myself off and headed her way. Destiny obviously had the same idea by having her fingers deep inside her own pussy. My lips parted, and my head tilted to the side. As I walked toward her, a whistle escaping my lips.

"Come here," I demanded, stroking my long and thick dick at the end of the bed. She knew exactly what to do. Pulling her fingers out of her pussy, she sucked her juices off of them, and then crawled toward me with her thick sexy ass.

She wasted no time grabbing ahold of my shit with her small, soft hands. She stroked it before covering it with spit and then devouring all ten of my inches with her full lips.

"Damn!" She had me howling like a bitch as she deep throated me.

"Mmmm. Mmmm." *Pop.* Destiny hummed, creating a vibrating sensation through me that I couldn't even explain before popping my shit out of her mouth. My cum smoothly glided down her throat, and she took every drop of it.

After she finished, I flipped her thick ass over onto her back. I hovered over her body and slid into her warm, wet, waiting pussy. I pounded her ass until I relieved all the stress from the day's work.

A Few Hours Later

I woke up to the smell of something that made my stomach growl. After all the weed and sex last night, I wouldn't mind something good to eat. I sat up, stretched, and then stood to take care of my hygiene before making my way to the kitchen.

I smacked Destiny on the ass as she stood there in a bra and thong, fixing our plates.

"Good morning, baby." She was the first to speak.

"Good morning, Des," I responded as I sat at the counter, waiting to be served.

After eating and listening to Destiny talk about her cousin moving back to Charlotte, it was time for her ass to go. I wasn't being mean or anything, but she'd served her purpose for the night. She knew how this thing with us went.

"Thank you for breakfast, baby. I'll call you," I said, dismissing her as I stood up to place my plate in the sink.

She placed her hand on her hip and the other on the counter and asked, "I thought we could spend the day together?"

"Come on, now. I got shit to do," I let her know. I hated when she tried to hang around when I needed to be somewhere.

She turned back around, mumbling, "OK."

She finished the dishes before getting dressed and leaving. She didn't say not one word to me, but I didn't give a damn. I just grabbed my stash before rolling up and lighting a blunt. I took a long pull, held it in, and then blew it out.

I looked around for my phone and realized I left it in the room. I stood to go get it and saw my brother's name flash across the screen.

"What's up, Reeno?" I answered.

"Yoooooo, wake ya ass up!"

"Nigga, I'm up. I had to kick Destiny's ass out, she talking about she want to spend the day with me. I swear I don't know what's wrong with these women." I took another pull of my blunt before leaning forward and putting it out in the ashtray.

"Yeah, OK, Raydon. You talking about me and A'Myracle, the same shit go for your ass." Reeno laughed at my expense.

"If you say so, nigga. What's up though, bruh?"

"Meet me off Tuck. We need to get Nelly's team back on track. I heard they were playing around last night." Reeno let me know.

That shit wasn't going to fly. Just because Nelly wasn't there, didn't mean them niggas didn't have to work.

"A'ight, I'll be there." I hung up the phone so that I could get ready to leave.

I pulled up to the small brick house on Tuckaseegee Road, which was one of our trap houses. Up and down the street you saw run-down homes with dead grass that needed cutting. My brother pulled up a few minutes after I did.

The guys that were outside scattered like roaches, going inside the house, acting as if they weren't fuckin' around this whole time. Wasn't nobody stupid though.

"What the fuck y'all niggas doing?" Reeno seethed at the sight of the four niggas pretending as if they were breaking down product.

"We working, boss man," Johnny, the head of the house answered.

"Nigga, y'all ran up in here when you saw us."

Reeno pulled his gun out because he didn't play with these dumb mothafuckas. Wasn't no one blind in this bitch.

"Now, let us ask again. What the fuck were y'all doing, hmm? Y'all playing around with our money? Hmm? What is it, nigga?" Reeno's nostrils flared as his left eye protruded, waiting on Johnny to say the wrong thing.

"We were waiting on Nelly. We haven't heard from him since yesterday," the nigga, Leroy answered, when he saw Johnny's ass couldn't from the way his mouth hung open in response to my gun in his fucking face.

My brother let them know that Nelly was a thief and was no longer with us. Of course, Leroy's ass questioned what exactly that statement meant. But I mean, how dumb can one be not to know what that shit meant?

I was up on Leroy in two seconds, smacking him across the face with my gun. I didn't like when someone questioned us. None of them knew the business like we did.

"Man, I was just asking. I didn't mean no harm," Leroy responded, holding the side of his face, which was bleeding.

"Well, next time, don't ask any questions. Now listen, that nigga is gone. Take that shit how you want to. For now, you guys will share the responsibility of this house equally. Either me or Reeno will be popping in periodically to check on things. When we see fit, we will put one of you, or maybe someone else in charge. Is that understood?" I looked over at each one of those fools who were glaring back at me, wanting to say some bullshit but knew not to.

All of them nodded in understanding. Reeno and I had to go over the way the house was run to each of them. Thankfully, everyone seemed to understand, so me and my brother went on our way after warning the four of them not to fuck up.

Chapter 2

Destiny

Two weeks later

I hadn't seen or heard from Raydon since he basically kicked me out of his place. I couldn't stand his ass sometimes, but I loved him in the same breath. I just didn't understand him. It's like, his feelings were on while he was deep in my pussy, but as soon as he pulled out, he had no feelings at all. I didn't know what was up with that.

If you ask me, I am a good catch, the type of woman that Raydon needed on his arm. I am fly as fuck, wearing a size fourteen, and I wear that shit proudly. Can't nobody call me fat, big-boned, none of that, because I am very confident in my own skin. I have smooth, butterscotch skin that covers the curves of my body. He definitely loved my full lips. He told me that my lips felt good against every part of his body.

It wasn't only my physical that was attractive, but my whole persona. I'm a classy chick. I owned my own home, car, and whatever else I had. I owned my own a real estate agency, and I was one of the best real estate agents in town, so I didn't want for nothing.

One thing I did know was that Raydon had better get his shit together before I started giving this good pussy to someone else who deserved it. Any other nigga would love to have a chick like me. A chick who could provide for herself and not have to depend on any man. A woman who he could surprise with gifts when he saw fit and not because she was nagging his ass for things.

The strong aroma of bleach permeated through the air as I made sure my house was clean from top to bottom. I was making sure everything was nice for my cousin, Eden, who just graduated from UNC Chapel Hill. She was coming to live with me for a while. I had three spare bedrooms; so of course, I didn't have a problem with her being here.

My phone rang, causing me to walk over to the kitchen counter. Seeing that it was Raydon's name on the caller ID, my lips curled up at the corners as I hit the ignore button on his ass. I placed my phone right back down and continued doing what I was doing. I didn't know what he wanted, nor did I care.

I made my way to the bathroom to shower after finishing up my cleaning. I took a quick one and then dressed in a pair of simple flowered tights, a blue shirt, and a pair of royal blue Vans.

As soon as I sat down in the living room to watch TV, the doorbell rang, followed by knocking. I rolled my eyes, thinking that it was Raydon's ass since he called two more times without me answering. However, when I opened the door, I was thrilled to see Eden.

"Oh my goodness! I missed you so much, cuz." I pulled her into my embrace, on the verge of crying. I'd only seen Eden a handful of times since she left for college. Before then, we were thick as thieves. If you saw one of us, you saw the both of us.

Our childhood was complicated. Our mothers were sisters who didn't want kids. They dealt with us because they had to. Since I am the oldest, I took on taking care of the two of us when I was just fifteen years old, and Eden was eleven. We never knew our fathers, and it's sad to say that our mothers were dead to us as soon as we were old enough to legally be on our own.

"I missed you too, sweetie. Thanks for letting me stay with you. I can't wait to hit the streets, cousin. We are going to get into everything." My cousin excitedly jumped up and down, shooting off statement after statement.

I helped her gather her bags out of her older model Honda Accord, that smelled like smoke, parked in my driveway.

"Girl, as soon as you get a job and situated, I'ma need you to get a new car." I frowned.

"Don't be talking about, Betsy. She has been through a lot."

I laughed at the fact that she named her car some damn Betsy. It does sound like an old woman though, so I guess it fits. We laughed all the way up the stairs as Eden decided on the room she would settle in.

My phone kept ringing, and of course, Eden's nosy ass wanted to know who it was. I pretty much just let her know that it was no one important before changing the subject.

For the next hour, we emptied Eden's suitcases and put her things away. It was nice catching up with my cousin. I was so happy that she was back.

Chapter 3

Reeno

My brother and I owned a car dealership where we sold used ˙ cars. It was really more my thing though. Raydon showed up when he needed to. We have our auction license where we could attend police auctions and bid on cars, allowing us to purchase them for dirt cheap and resell them for a higher price after we made the necessary fixes that the cars may have needed. The car selling business had proven to be a profitable one.

I strode into the building and spoke to the receptionist, Angel, who was sitting at her desk, sipping on a cup of coffee.

"Hey, Reeno, baby. You want me to fix you a cup?" She beamed as she held her cup of coffee up.

"Nah, I'm good today."

I continued to my office but didn't get to get in there good before Angel came in complaining about some dudes that looked like trouble in the parking lot.

"Their guns are showing and everything."

"A'ight, when I leave out, place the magnet lock on the door for me."

Angel nodded her head in understanding as I reached under my desk to pull my gun out, chamber a bullet, and head out the door. It was one thing I didn't fool around with, and that was my fucking businesses.

I scoped them niggas out, taking long strides to get to where they stood. They definitely looked out of place, like they were some out of town niggas. I didn't know what they wanted with me, but they were barking up the wrong tree.

"Can I help y'all with something?"

I figured the nigga standing in front was the leader. Not once did I lose eye contact with him. He eventually responded to my question by saying, "Nah, ain't shit here, son."

His flunkies called themselves snickering, but I didn't find shit funny, nor did I have time for the bullshit.

"Get the fuck off of my property then, nigga," I warned as I removed my gun from my waist.

The nigga observed the way my finger was inching toward the trigger, as he responded, "Yes, we will leave for now, but you better believe that I will be back." He and his flunkies then turned, walking away.

I really didn't give a damn if they came back or not. One thing was for sure though, the niggas wouldn't be leaving alive if they did come back. I waited until the little hooptie they were riding in pulled off before going back inside the building once Angel unlocked the door.

I walked into my office, shutting the door. I put my gun back on safety and placed it back under my desk. I laid my head back against my tall brown chair and closed my eyes. I was wracking my brain, trying to figure out who those niggas were but was coming up empty.

"What's up, NaToya?" My head popped up, and I frowned when I realized someone opened my door without me telling their asses to come in. I didn't feel like dealing with her right now, and she knew not to pop her ass up.

"I figured you wanted something to eat." She placed the Styrofoam container on my wooden desk.

I was grateful that she thought enough about me to bring me something to eat, because I hadn't eaten anything all day.

"Thanks, ToyToy, but you know how I feel about you popping up on a nigga."

I stood up, grabbing her and then pulling her close to me. I knew her fucking panties were wet by the way her sexy ass was biting her lip. My hand went under her skirt and inside her panties, dipping my finger inside to confirm what I already knew.

"I know, but I haven't seen you, and I missed you so much," she moaned as I continued my assault on her pussy with my fingers.

After she came, I turned her around and trapped her in my muscular arms by placing them on the desk.

"Thank you for the food, baby." I placed my hands on her thick thighs. Between her and A'Myracle, they kept me busy.

"What you really come here for, hun?" I licked my lips, knowing exactly what she wanted.

Without saying a word, she backed my ass up to the wall as she unbuckled my pants. This bitch wanted my ass bad, and who was I to deny her?

Once she got my shit down, she squatted and demolished my dick.

"Oh shit, Toy." My hands went through her short hair as she went to work.

NaToya slurped and sucked my shit like she missed the big mothafucka for real. It didn't take long for my seeds to go spraying down her throat. As I was still squirting with my eyes closed and head back, my door opened causing NaToya to pull away, and caused my semen to hit NaToya's chest. My eyes popped open when I heard Angel's voice.

"Damn."

This girl didn't even try to turn around, cover her eyes, or nothing. Angel was damn near drooling with no shame. I knew her ass wanted me, now she was really going to be tripping.

"Bitch, don't you see me sucking his dick?" NaToya boldly stated with much attitude.

I couldn't do nothing but laugh at her crazy ass. Then Angel's smart-ass mouth said, "Yeah, I see your hoe ass."

"Get out, Angel," I sternly said, because I didn't play that shit. Neither one of these hoes needed to be fighting over me.

Angel took one last look at my dick with her petty ass and left out of my office after she told me I had a customer.

NaToya tried to tell me to check Angel, but who did she think she was? She damn shole didn't run shit over here. I dismissed her ass so I could get myself together and handle my business.

I made sure everything was straight, and I was on point before I opened my door and exited to see a man dressed as if he had money. This was what I liked to see, someone about they own business.

"How may I help you today?" I asked him.

"Hey man, I was interested in a few cars up front. My twins just got their license and have been begging me for cars. Daddy got to do what Daddy got to do."

"I feel you, man. Let's go see what we can get your kids into today."

******

I quickly did everything I needed to do in order to shut business down for the day. I called my brother, letting him know what went down, and he agreed to meet me at our parents' house.

It took me a minute to get to my parents' home since they decided to live on the lake. Their shit was bigger than a mothafucka. My father wouldn't have it any other way. I pulled around the circular driveway after keying in the code to the gate.

A smile spread across my face when I saw my mother fucking with her plants and shit out front. I quickly made it her way to hug my queen. "What up, Ma?"

Arleene, better known as Leena, was just as beautiful as she could be. Her brown skin glowed, and her smile could light up the saddest person's world. I knew my father had a lot to do with that shit. I imagined someone like her when I was ready to settle down. My mother was smart as fuck. Her and my father met when she went to Spelman, and he was across the way at Morehouse. Stanford saw her ambition from the beginning; beauty and brains.

"Hello, son." My mother stood to her feet and reached up to give me a kiss on the cheek.

"Let's go inside so I can check on this food. Where is your brother?" She glanced over at me as I held the front door open for her.

"That nigga on his way."

She stopped in her tracks and looked back at me with the evil eye. I could only smile at her cute self. I knew my Leena would still knock me upside the head at twenty-nine years old, so I threw my hands up and apologized. Her old ass hated the word nigga.

We finally made it to the kitchen where my momma washed her hands and then dried them. She then applied a little hand sanitizer, rubbing her hands together. She then lifted her apron off the counter and tied it around her body.

My stomach growled once my momma opened that oven. The smell itself had me wanting to skip this damn meeting, but it was necessary. We had to know what was going on. I tried my luck to see what it was, but my hand got popped before it even made it to the corner of the aluminum foil.

"Gone, boy."

Leena had an attitude as always when someone tried to touch her food. See, my momma was playing games today. She opened the refrigerator and pulled out a plate of homemade macadamia nut and chocolate chip cookies. She had to make both because I fucks with the macadamia nuts, but Raydon fucks with the chocolate chips.

"Here, you can have one." My momma unwrapped the cookies and then handed me the plate that held the macadamia nut.

"I see how it is, Ma. You feeding this nigga cookies and not me?" Raydon walked into the kitchen.

His ass got that same look she gave me before saying, "I swear y'all asses spoiled. Get your damn cookie and get out of here."

We both kissed her before heading down the hallway to our father's home office.

"What's up, old man?" Raydon greeted my father.

"Nigga, I'm tired of telling you that I'm not too old to whip your ass. You better tell him, Reeno."

"What I have to tell him that shit for like you beat my ass before or something?" I said, causing Stanford to snort.

This was an ongoing argument. My father always thought he could beat somebody's ass. His old, weak-boned ass didn't realize that he didn't have the juice anymore. His ass was not in his prime anymore. He was way past that shit.

"Yeah, OK. But what's this about someone coming to the dealership?" Stanford questioned.

"Some niggas call themselves sending a message of some sort, but all they said was that they'd be back." I repeated what happened.

We all tried to put our heads together and think about who had beef with us, but no one could think of one soul. My brother and I treated niggas like they were family, for real. If they needed anything, we were there. We paid everyone heftily, so no one should have a problem.

My father agreed to speak with the guys from the police force that we had on payroll to see if anyone knew who was in town. After that, we all stood to go see what my momma cooked up in the kitchen.

My brother wanted to hit the club later, which was cool with me. I fucked up that cheese and broccoli stuffed chicken my mother cooked. It was nothing like her cooking. My future wife definitely needed to know how to put it down.

Chapter 4

Destiny

I felt the most jovial feeling when Raydon invited me out to his father's lounge. I thought it was his way of apologizing for basically dismissing me the last time we saw each other like I was a common hoe. I couldn't wait to show up in an outfit so hot that it would not only turn his head but others too.

I was sitting at my vanity, applying makeup when Eden came sashaying her petite, pretty ass up in my room. I loved the brown shorts that seemed to be painted onto her petite frame. It made her look as if she had a round ass. The orange four-inch stilettos looked like they hurt her feet, but it cost to be cute.

"Damn, girl. I know we going to find you a man tonight."

"Look at you though, Destiny. That dress is riding up your thighs. That shit cute though."

My see-through black dress with the sides cut out was sure to bring attention to me. I had nothing under it but a black bra and panty set. I was showing out for real, but I knew what I was doing.

"Come on, boo; let me do your makeup. I'll put you a light coat with some glitter on your eyelids." I stood up so that Eden could sit down. She spun around on the stool so that she was facing me, and I beat her face to the gods, as they say. Once we checked ourselves out in the mirror, we were out the door. We were some badass females and ready for the night.

We decided to take my Nissan Altima since it was the best out of our two cars. The ride over to Chill Lounge was filled with both

Eden and I catching up more on our lives. I was so glad to have my cousin back.

The parking lot looked full to capacity when I pulled in. I found a parking space, and we headed inside. Of course, we were turning heads as we made our way to the front of the line that was wrapped around the brick building.

I walked right up to the big black bouncer and gave him my name. He knew exactly who I was and directed me to our V.I.P section.

"Damn, Destiny. So you know the guy who owns this place?" Eden asked me as we sauntered to our spot.

"Not really. It's his father's place, but he and his brother share some of the responsibilities."

Eden nodded her head as we sat down to wait for Raydon. In the process, a waitress came up and introduced herself.

"Hey, my name is A'Myracle. I was sent over to take care of you guys. What would you ladies like to drink tonight?"

I remembered that this girl messed around with Raydon's brother, Reeno. She had a fake smile plastered on her face. As long as she didn't come at us wrong, she was good. I may have had everything going for myself, but I would still bust a bitch on her ass if need be.

Eden and I were Cîroc girls, so I informed her that we wanted that.

"Do you have vanilla?" Eden inquired as she swayed to the music, watching the exotic dancer on stage.

"Yes, I will get that for you along with juice, ice, and glasses for you to mix your drinks." A'Myracle then turned on her heels to walk away.

"Thank you!" I yelled toward her back, in which she threw up her hand rudely.

Eden and I talked for a minute about Raydon, and then the waitress came back over with our drinks.

I was mixing our drinks when I felt someone's dick poking in my ass. I was about to turn around swinging until I heard his sexy ass voice say, "What up, Destiny?"

My ass was grinning like hell as I turned around to face him, giving him a hug. Raydon looked sexy as always in a pair of denim jeans and a button-up with sneakers. It didn't take much for him to turn heads.

"Hey, babe." He kissed my cheek, and then that's when he noticed what I had on.

He had the cutest frown on his face, and it was just the reaction that I was looking for.

"The fuck ya ass got on, Des?"

I smiled at him as I turned around, giving him a three-sixty view. His eyes looked murderous, yet lustful as he eyed me. I looked over at Eden and winked my eye, which caused her to smirk.

"You know you getting it tonight, right? Coming out of the house like that. Fuck wrong wit' you?" He pulled me back close to him and then eyed Eden.

"Babe, this is my cousin, Eden, I told you about. Eden, this is Raydon."

Raydon held out his hand, and Eden shook it saying, "Nice to meet you."

"Likewise, Eden." Raydon grabbed her hand, squeezing it gently.

By this time, Reeno was walking up, and I noticed Eden with her eyes wide open and glued to him. I was not sure if those two would mesh well, but judging by the way he was staring her down, I was sure we were about to see.

"What up, Destiny. Who is this beauty?" Reeno reached over, giving me a side hug before continuing to say, "Who is this beauty with you tonight?"

"This is my cousin, Eden. Eden, this is Raydon's brother, Reeno."

I watched them for a minute until Raydon caught my attention by grabbing my chin, turning it toward him. I knew this damn dress would get it poppin'. He just didn't want another nigga all over me like that.

"Come with me." He grabbed my hand and was about to pull me out of VIP, but I stopped him, wanting to make sure my cousin was OK with this.

"Eden, you OK if I go with Raydon for a minute?"

Her ass smirked as she nodded her head. She knew what was up and wouldn't cock block on her cousin. Raydon then led me out of V.I.P and to a private room.

His ass thought he was slick. He wanted some of this kitty cat knowing it would keep me from messing around with someone else. Once in the room, Raydon gently pushed me down on the couch and lifted my dress up to my waist. He fell to his knees and began to lap my juices up after ripping my panties. His face was buried deep in my pussy until I exploded.

I laid there breathing hard, legs shaking and all, in anticipation until he released himself and pulled me up, leading me to the wall.

He placed my back against it and then lifted my leg up, placing it on his right shoulder. I may be a little big, but I was flexible as hell. He gently entered me before easing in and out of my canal.

"Oh my god, Raydon," I moaned as he picked up his pace. His balls were slapping against my leg while I moved my hips, trying to keep up with him. Raydon didn't play that stiff shit; we got it in every time. He licked my leg as he pounded my pussy, causing me to cum instantly as my juices ran down my trembling leg.

"Damn, girl." He bit his bottom lip.

Raydon grunted as he pulled out of me, and I leaned over the couch so that he could finish his nut. Once he did, we washed up as well as we could, and then joined the others in the club. When we walked up, my cousin looked upset. What the fuck was going on that fast?

Eden

Shit, who was this fine specimen walking toward us. He just strode over in his tailored suit as if he owned the place. The small mole underneath his eye made him look even sexier.

A cigar hung between his thick lips before he took a puff to release the smoke into the air and then held the cigar between his fingers. Even the way he was smoking this cigar was sexy to me. They definitely didn't have men like him back in school.

When Destiny informed me that he was Raydon's brother, I could see the resemblance. They favored but were different in many ways.

My palms were sweaty as he lifted my hand to kiss the back of it. His soft lips caused a tingle in between my thighs and my bottom lip to sink between my teeth.

"What's up, pretty lady?" His smooth, deep voice resonated through my ears.

"Hey." I giggled like a schoolgirl.

I walked toward the loveseat and sat down, crossing one long leg across the other. I could see him follow my every move before following and sitting down himself. I cutely sipped my drink, getting into the music when I felt this fool's hand on my thigh. Now he had me fucked up. I didn't know him like that.

He laughed as I smacked his hand away like the shit was funny.

"Damn, you feisty." He chuckled as he smashed his cigar inside the ashtray on the table in front of him.

"I'm not; I just don't know you to be feeling all on me and shit." I let his ass know I didn't play that shit. He would have to come at me with respect if he wanted to talk to me.

"You can get to know me, baby, because I damn sure want to get to know you." He was damn near undressing me with those deep brown, sexy eyes of his. That mole moving up and down along with his cheeks did something to me.

My teeth bore down into my lip, and my leg was bouncing up and down to keep from smacking his ass. I smacked my lips, glancing at him out the corner of my eyes. He was still smiling, getting on my damn nerves. He was already starting off wrong. I could see that he was one of those types that thought because he had money, that he could do and say whatever he wanted. Well, his ass had met the right one today.

"You know what…" I said as I stood up, placing my drink on the table.

I turned around, spotting my cousin walking back into the V.I.P area, so I grabbed her arm, telling her to come on.

"What's wrong, Eden?" She looked back at Reeno who was now laughing with Raydon. I stuck up my middle finger as we continued to the bathroom.

I walked into the bathroom, placing my hands on the sink with my head down. I took a few deep breaths, trying not to be angry.

"What happened, cuz? Do I need to go back in there and whip somebody's ass?" Destiny asked, which made me look up at her, rolling my eyes.

"Maybe if you weren't off fucking, he wouldn't have tried me like he did. Damn, girl, you left me with some nigga I don't know, in a place I don't know, just to get your rocks off?"

I could tell I hurt her feelings, but I didn't care right now. That was crazy of her to do. I didn't care if she asked for my permission or not. She knew I wasn't going to tell her ass no, especially when she looked so happy to be in that nigga's presence.

"I don't understand what happened Eden; I would never do anything to hurt you."

I could hear the sincerity in Destiny's voice. I knew she wouldn't hurt me. I was just upset.

"He is just arrogant as fuck. He call himself trying to feel on my leg. I don't know his ass like that." I felt my face frown up.

Destiny frowned at me before just leaving the bathroom. I called out to her, but she kept on walking. I didn't want to start anything, but I should have known because she is a firecracker.

"Raydon, you better get your disrespectful ass brother!" I heard Destiny scream as I was rushing up the stairs. She was up in Reeno's face, and of course, he held a smirk on his face. He wasn't thinking nothing about what my cousin was talking about. This really made me mad at his ass.

Raydon pulled her away, pretty much letting her know to mind her business. It was actually funny because she actually did what he said, causing a frown to show on my face.

Reeno's eyes were back on me again, licking his sexy ass lips.

"You finish talking shit about me, Ms. Pretty?"

"Boy, bye. Nobody has time to talk about your ass." Destiny answered before I could.

"Didn't I tell your ass to mind your business? Let her handle her own," Raydon demanded.

"It's a'ight, bro. Destiny lying anyway. I know Ms. Eden was thinking about me. I can smell her pussy from over here."

My mouth opened, and my eyes widened, but I didn't have a comeback. I turned and left V.I.P, going over to the bar. The girl, A'Myracle, was there, and I asked her for a drink. As soon as she placed it down, a gentleman sat beside me, grabbing my attention. His neatly twisted locks were up in a bun. He had tattoos that covered his right arm and hand. It was sexy.

"Hey, how are you?"

My eyes moved from his head to his feet before I responded, "I'm great. How are you?"

"I'm good, shawty. My name is Suave. What's yours?"

"Taken."

My head snapped back, and my face scrunched up, looking at Reeno who had the nerve to be standing with his back toward me with his right hand planted on the bar.

"My bad, Reeno. If she would have told me she was taken, I would have backed off," Suave's punk ass said.

"But I'm not hi…" I tried to say, but Reeno turned his head, giving me a *shut the fuck up* look.

Suave then shook Reeno's hand and walked away. Reeno was playing games. He was trying to check me, but I saw this chick behind the bar giving him the side eye.

"Don't try to play me. I don't even know you, and you already acting a fool. Imagine if I let you get to know me."

"Let's get this straight." Reeno walked up so close that I could smell the masculine smell of his cologne.

"You can't let me do shit, pretty lady. I do what I want. And what I'm going to do is put this dick in you and straighten out that mouth of yours."

Next thing I knew, his wet lips were on my neck before he stood up straight and walked away. I truly didn't know what I was going to do about this man. But something told me that I was stuck with his ass.

Reeno

Most of these women were the same in some way. I could tell that baby girl wasn't with bullshit, but I could also tell she wanted to give me the pussy. I laughed at the thought as I watched her storm out of the club.

"That's how you doing it?"

I turned with a frown on my face toward A'Myracle. She was definitely in her feelings.

"What you talking about, damn?"

"You are really starting to disrespect me. You claiming that hoe like you know her."

"Aye, you know I don't play this shit. Get at me when you get your feelings in check."

I walked off from her ass. She was yelling something about needing to talk to me about something important, but I didn't want to hear that shit.

I let my brother know that I was out and headed toward the back of the place where I parked my car. I pulled out and headed to the gas station for some shit I needed.

"What up, Reeno?"

Some nigga who I recognized worked for me spoke as I was entering. It was damn near 2 a.m., and I wasn't about to be caught slippin' with all that was going on. I spoke to him but kept it moving. I grabbed a Dr. Pepper, the purple pack of skittles, and headed to the register to get my White Owls.

The same nigga was outside once I stepped outside those sliding doors. I still kept walking. I glanced behind me as I removed the gas nozzle, placing the nozzle inside my gas tank, and squeezing the handle.

"Is there a reason you up in my space and shit?" I finally turned around, tired of his ass just staring at me.

This nigga didn't move a muscle for a minute like he was thinking hard about what he was wanting to say.

"Come on, nigga. I don't have all day." I pulled the gas nozzle out, replacing it back in its place.

"Yeah, uhm, I've been looking for Nelly, but it seems he disappeared or something. I know I'm probably risking my life by stepping to you. Have you seen him?"

I stood straight up, cocking my head to the side with my arms folded across my chest. I had no idea why this lil' nigga thought it was OK to be in my business on some bullshit that had nothing to do with him.

"What's your name, youngin?"

"Lonny, man."

"Well, Lonny, it's obvious that you know who I am."

"Yeah, I know who you are. Everyone does, and everyone is saying that you had something to do with Nelly's disappearance."

My hands dropped to my side as I looked at this nigga through hooded eyes. My face burned red as I suddenly snatched this Lonny character up by the collar of his white T-shirt and jacked him up against the grimy post beside the gas pump. I gritted my teeth at this lame and warned him. "If you know who I am, then you know not to ask me no got damn question like that. When I let you go, I advise you to go post back up on that dingy little wall you were on, and sell my shit."

I then yanked him forward and let him go, shoving his ass back. Lonny's ass was lucky today. It was too many eyes around to do what I wanted to do, which was beat his ass for being in my business.

"Yes, sir." Lonny turned around with his head hung low, walking back to the brick wall he was previously standing on.

I definitely had to keep an eye on this dude. I didn't trust someone who asked questions that had nothing to do with them.

******

The next morning, I was up and at it early. I had to swing by the car lot and check up on things before heading to my real destination. I chuckled as I pulled up to Destiny's house. I saw my brother's car, which I hated because I knew his ass was going to have something to say.

I stepped out of my truck and walked up the walkway that was surrounded by some big ass elephant ears. I only knew about those shits 'cause my mother had them in her yard.

"Hey, Reeno, what are you doing here?" Destiny inquired, opening up the door in a pajama pantsuit.

"You know why I'm here." I gave her a devilish smile.

Destiny frowned at me before a smile graced her face.

"Babe, who is that?" I heard my brother before I saw him walk up behind Destiny. Raydon chortled when he noticed it was me.

"Fuck you doing popping up at my girl's house? Let that nigga in, babe," Raydon told Destiny, making her open the door wider so that I could fit through it.

I walked in and stood in her foyer area as I said, "I don't even want to hear the shit. Y'all know what it is. She still sleeping or something?" I asked once I saw that Eden wasn't downstairs or anything.

"Reeno, Eden is going to be so mad at me if I let you up there."

Destiny tried to stop me as I turned and continued to go up the carpeted stairs. If she didn't want to let me know which room, then I would find that shit myself. Destiny should've known by now that I was just like my damn brother; I did what I wanted to do.

"Reeno, stop," Destiny pleaded.

"Let that man handle his business, baby," I heard Raydon whisper.

I chuckled as I continued on my journey to find my future woman. There was only one door that was shut upstairs, so I had a feeling that that was the room that I would find Eden in. I carefully turned the knob and pushed the door open. Once I stepped in, I closed the door back, then turned my body around to admire her.

The sheet she had over the lower half of her body barely covered her ass. I licked my lips, glancing at her succulent breasts. She had just enough for me to squeeze while licking her tiny nipples.

I felt like a stalker standing here, and for what I was about to do. I removed my shoes and laid down on the empty side of the bed, facing her. I knew this girl was about to go off on me as soon as she saw me. I shook her gently while saying, "Ms. Eden, baby."

Her eyes fluttered, but she didn't immediately wake up. I shook her again while calling her name, and that's when her eyes popped open, and she screamed at the top of her lungs.

"What the fuck are you doing in here?" Her strong ass pushed my big ass out of the bed and then hurriedly pulled the sheet over her body.

I heard laughter and turned my head toward the door to see Raydon peeking through.

"Get the fuck out of here," I said, getting up off the floor.

"Fuck you, stalking ass nigga," Raydon joked as he closed the door.

I sat in the recliner chair away from her violent ass. I couldn't contain the way my eyes jumped around her pretty ass face. Her nose scrunched up, and her eyebrows dipped. It was cute. I laughed at her ass.

"Ms. Eden."

"Mr. Stalker."

"I ain't no fucking stalker. I just want what I want, Ms. Eden."

The minute her ass blushed, I knew she wanted my ass too. She wanted me to chase her ass. That's what the problem was.

"Reeno, get out so I can at least put some clothes on."

"Nah, I'm not bothering you."

"Oooo, you make me sick." She got up and secured the sheet around her body before grabbing a pair of shorts and a shirt, along with underclothes and headed to the bathroom inside of her room. I laughed, hearing the locks turn on the door. I wasn't even going to mess with her little ass. I folded my arms as I sat back in the chair, getting comfortable to wait on her.

I must have drifted off to sleep, because I felt a kick to my leg, causing me to jump up.

"What's up, Ms. Eden?" I stared up at her with her hand on her petite hip, her attitude on full display.

"What do you want from me? You don't even know me, and you are already stalking me. What happened to courting a woman the old-fashioned way?"

"I'm not old-fashioned, Eden. I'm a boss. I get what I want." I stood to my feet and walked toward her. My hand fell to her waist as my other hand traced her jawline. I felt her quiver to my touch, and that shit made my day.

"You are beautiful, and I just want to get to know you. Let me take you out, and if you don't enjoy yourself, then I will think about leaving you alone." I was dead ass too, but her ass burst out laughing. Before she was able to say anything else, Raydon began beating on the door like he was getting robbed or some shit.

"Bruh, we have to go. Code red, my nigga."

At the sound of that, I let go of Eden, put my shoes back on my feet, and bolted to the door. I turned around for a second and kissed her lips before disappearing for real.

"Really, nigga?"

I didn't have time to comment on what she screamed. I just kept it moving. I would just have to explain later. Code red meant that there was someone fucking with our money, and a possible robbery in progress. Both me and my brother hopped in our trucks and peeled out of Destiny's driveway.

We pulled up to the house off Boswell Rd. The area was eerily quiet. It was nothing but old heads and crackheads that roamed this neighborhood. It must've been scarce because of what went down. My Nikes hit the pavement before I stood up straight and shut my truck door. I made my way to the house directly across the street, and to the guy who called us house.

"What's good, Earl?" I held out my hand, and Earl shook it before he said, "Just trying to make it out here, man."

"I feel you, so run-down to me what happened. I know you and Raydon only spoke briefly on the phone."

Earl told me what happened in its entirety. I reached in my pocket when he was finished, and peeled off a thousand dollars, handing it to Earl.

"I really do appreciate it, man. I'm going to go over here and see what the damage is. I'll holla at you," I stated before turning around and heading to my trap house.

As soon as I walked through the door, I became upset. I walked through the whole house and it was ransacked. All of my product and money was gone, and what wasn't taken was spread throughout the house as if the plastic was torn, and the packages were thrown around. Tables and couches were turned over and everything.

I noticed my brother in the living room, standing over an unconscious Dave.

"No one else is in here. Where are Warren, Letrell, and Vernon?" My eyes moved around the living room, assessing the damage from the intruders. Like I said before, this shit was terrible.

"Not here," my brother responded.

I saw a white bucket filled with ice cold water, which Raydon picked up and threw it on Dave. He gasped, throwing his fists in the air, trying to catch his breath. When he looked up and saw me, he was somewhat relieved. I watched as Dave looked around as if he was trying to figure out where he was. He then sat up and said, "Them niggas said you took something from them, and they are going to take everything from you."

I shared a look with my brother, wondering what the fuck we could have taken from someone. We weren't the type to take, but to give. A nigga was really confused.

"Did they say what it was we supposedly took?" I questioned Dave, and he immediately shook his head no.

I kicked a small wooden table over as I screamed obscenities. This shit just didn't make sense.

After calming down, I let Dave go and instructed him to take a few days to get himself together. Before he left, he let us know one last thing.

"I heard one of the guys say that they no longer worked for you, but for them. I swear we tried to take them, but they came from all directions. They were prepared like they knew the layout of the house," Dave said as he held on to the side of his bleeding head.

At this point, there had to be a snake in the camp somewhere. We hadn't had any issues this whole time. We respected our workers and paid them more than enough. That was why we didn't have any idea on where to start.

******

It was late when I pulled into my designated parking spot. Unlike Raydon, I preferred living in a building, preferably the penthouse. With security, I felt as if I could keep a handle on unwanted visitors. Only people who could get to my place right now are my brother and my parents.

Stepping off the elevator, I headed straight to the bathroom to relieve myself and then shower. I stood under the shower head as the water beat down on my skin at maximum power. The shit felt good. I closed my eyes for a second. I needed the stress of the situation to go down the drain with the water.

As I washed myself, I thought about Eden; sexy and feisty Eden. Times like these, I wish I had a woman to come home to. Eden would be perfect if I could get her ass to cooperate.

After I finished up in the bathroom, I went to the kitchen to grab a Bud Light before retiring in my room for the night. I twisted the top off the beer, and took a sip, letting out a loud belch before I grabbed my phone and dialed Eden's number.

The phone rang four times before her sexy, sluggish voice resonated through the speaker. "Hello." It sounded like she answered more as a question than a statement.

I took another sip of my beer and sat it on the table next to my bed. I then laid on my back with my right arm behind my head, holding on to the phone with my left.

"What's up, Ms. Eden?"

She sucked her teeth and said, "Yes, Reeno." She sounded aggravated that I was calling her at almost two in the morning, but I didn't give a fuck.

"Damn, earlier your panties and shit was getting wet. Now you have an attitude?"

"You know what? I can't with you. You need to learn to talk to a woman. I'm not one of these thirsty hoes out here. The shit is not cute. Plus, it's two in the morning, and I have a job interview to go to in a few hours."

I wasn't used to a woman checking my ass, but for some reason, Eden made that shit sexy.

"I'm sorry. Let's try this again. I definitely don't want you feeling disrespected. I want you on my side, Eden."

"Yeah, I hear you." I heard her smack her lips. I chuckled, imagining her rolling her eyes too.

"Destiny said you just moved back home. Where were you?"

"I went to Carolina," she responded.

"Oh, for real? A Tar Heels Alumni; I can dig it. What did you study?"

"Biology and education. I'm going to be a science teacher." I could tell she was excited about what she had accomplished. Shit, I was too, and I had no problem letting her know.

"That's dope as fuck. I see you got a good head on your shoulders. I like that shit."

"Thank you." Eden accepted my compliment.

"I see that got a smile on your face."

"And I see you finally got some sense." Eden giggled, causing me to chuckle.

We were both silent for a few seconds before I finally said, "I'm coming to get you tomorrow after your interview."

"How you know I want to go somewhere with you?" she questioned.

"Oh, you do," I stated confidently.

"I'll see you tomorrow. Say bye."

"Bye," Eden said, and we both hung up.

Chapter 5

Warren

I slowly peeled my eyes open and observed the water stained ceilings, which probably came from leaks when it rained or when the pipes burst. I turned my head to the right, seeing the chipped wallpaper and old paint. I looked down at the old worn out couch I was on that smelled of urine. I sucked in a deep breath as a huge water bug crawled over my arm. I hated those shits, especially when they get to flying.

My eyes diverted around the room, noticing Vernon and Latrell, who also appeared to be just thrown down on an old mattress and a chair. I stood to my feet, struggling at first. I gathered myself and limped over to Latrell, who was the closest to me. I shook my head, feeling a little woozy like I'd been drugged or some shit. I was trying to remember what happened, but only bits and pieces came to me.

I shook Latrell, who suddenly jumped up and backed up to the wall.

"It's me, man," I whispered, being sure to keep eye contact with him.

Latrell looked around in a panic, which woke Vernon up as well.

"We have to get out of here," Latrell began, looking around, I'm guessing in search of a way to escape.

"Bro, there are no windows or anything up in this place," I told him.

Latrell went up the stairs and tried turning the knob. When it wouldn't open, he started panicking and yanking on the knob.

"Stop, nigga, damn. You see the shit is locked. Reeno and Raydon will find us."

"Man, y'all really think them niggas is going to come for us? I mean, why would they care?" Latrell barged into my thoughts.

"You know they are loyal, Latrell," I answered, just as the basement door swung open and a dark-skinned, buff nigga walked through the door with three other niggas behind him.

"What the fuck y'all niggas doin'? Step the fuck back." The guy in front belted out as he lifted his foot and kicked Vernon in his kneecap.

"Ahhh, shit!" Vernon fell to the ground, holding his knee, squeezing his eyes tight.

"Stop being a bitch, my nigga," one of the other niggas said.

"Listen up; you niggas work for us now. Reeno and Raydon no longer exist to you. You will stay down here and cook up all of our product that we stole. When I feel like you can be trusted, then you will be able to go out."

None of us said anything. Once the guys left, I explained to the fellas that we had to play the part. We got to work and would be patiently waiting for the chance to escape or be rescued. Either way, that big black nigga had us fucked up.

Chapter 6

Raydon

As soon as Destiny started jiggling my balls with her hand, I exploded in her mouth.

"I can't get enough of your little ass. Lay on your fucking back, and them knees need to touch your ears. I want that pussy to fart when I ease up in there."

Without question, she did what I asked. Her knees were so far upward that she could barely breathe. I secured a condom on my dick, and my knees hit the mattress before tapping her clitoris. I was amazed at the fluid leaking out of her tiny hole. I then eased my huge tip in and out of her pussy until I felt like she was stretched enough to ease all the way in. As soon as my dick was in deep, her pussy farted.

"Uhn, hun, that's what I like to hear." I smacked the back of her leg hard as hell, causing her to yelp before I pulled out and entered her again rough as fuck.

I watched the different faces she was making as I murdered her pussy. She tried to push me back, telling me to slow down. She knew I didn't play that shit. I smacked her hand away, letting her know I wasn't wit' it.

"I get this shit the way I want it." I pulled out of her and snatched the condom off before lowering her legs and slid up in her raw.

"Oh my god, Raydon."

I had her ass screaming at the top of her lungs. I bent down to kiss her nastily before pulling out, having her get on her knees. I placed my left hand on her lower back as my right guided my thickness inside. I thrust forward while smacking her ass. I spread her butt cheeks so I could see what I was doing. My thumb went in her ass, causing her to scream out louder. Our skin was slapping together, and my balls hung low, waiting to be emptied into her pussy.

"Say my fucking name."

Smack.

"Now. Fuck." I went harder.

"Raydon, yes. Fuck me harder, baby."

I did what she asked, giving her long deep strokes. She matched my stroke until her body began to tremble. I reached down and toyed with her clit, causing her to explode. I pulled out, having the urge to suck on her clit, which is what I did. I didn't even give her ass time to recuperate.

Once I was filled up by her juices, I flipped her back onto her back and plunged into her. I kissed her shoulder and slow grinded my hips to the rhythm in my head. I licked the sweat from her round breasts as I felt my stomach tightening. She came again, and I was right behind her.

A nigga was breathing like I had asthma or some shit. Once I caught my breath, I pulled out slowly cause my dick was sensitive as fuck. I got up and helped her up, even though she could barely stand. We took a quick shower before ending up back in the bed. I pulled her back toward me and draped my arm over her waist as the cool air circulated around Destiny's bedroom.

When she turned, facing me, I had a feeling she was going to come with some bullshit.

"What are we doing, Raydon?"

She spoke softly, using her fingertips to caress my arms, and with her pretty eyes glaring back at me. I moved her hair out of her face with my fingers and asked, "What do you mean?"

"I mean exactly what I asked. I mean, we do shit together, we sleep together, and I feel we match each other. However, we are not together. I know you fucking other hoes. So again, what are we doing? I feel like I'm wasting my time."

I lifted up, holding myself up on my arm and asked, "Fuck you mean wasting your time?"

"Out of everything I said, that's what you respond to?" Her right brow was raised slightly as she sat up and closed her arms. She was acting like she was the one that was supposed to be upset. She was the one coming to me with this nonsense.

"I mean, you worried about the wrong shit, Destiny. As long as I give you time, I don't see what the issue is. Why you worried about who I'm fuckin'? We have what we have, baby. We working. So why fuck that up for a title, Des?" I stood abruptly and began pacing the floor.

I couldn't believe this girl was taking it there with me. All this time she made no indication that she had an issue with what we were doing. I didn't know who she had been talking to, but she needed to stop letting whoever fill her head with shit. Damn.

"That's how you really feel?"

Destiny hopped up right after me with teary eyes. I was really trying to figure out what the problem was. This girl was upset for no reason. For the first time in my life, my ass was confused as fuck.

"It's cool though. I see how you feel. Just remember you said that when I open my legs and let a real nigga get this wet pussy."

She said that shit and tried to walk off like I was just going to let her. Yeah, she has lost her mind. My nostrils flared as I glared at her ass. My teeth bore against each other when I looked at her through my protruding eyes. I couldn't contain myself listening to her spit that bullshit. Before I realized what I was doing, I had her ass hemmed up against the wall with my arm against her neck. Our noses were damn near touching as she struggled to remove my arm.

"What the fuck you just say to me; another nigga going to do what to my pussy? That's my pussy, you understand?" I loosened my grip on her so she could answer. Tears ran down her cheeks as she nodded.

"Get off of me, Raydon." She finally opened her mouth.

"Nah, I need you to understand this so there is no more confusion. I'm feeling you more than those other hoes. You get most of my time. I'm here for you in ways that I am not for them."

I used my right hand to lift her chin and pecked her lips a few times. I could feel her body reacting by the way her breath got caught in her throat. I lifted her body in my arms. Her legs circled my waist before I eased her down on what her body craved so much. I knew I fucked up by putting my hands on her, but she had to realize that she was mine no matter what.

Chapter 7

Reeno

I was sitting in my office at the dealership, my feet up on the desk, chillin'. A bullshit ass e-mail came through on my phone, and I was just done with all the shit.

I pulled the security tapes from when those guys showed up to the lot, fast-forwarding it to when they first arrived. I stared at the freeze frame, trying to see if I recognized any of them. I sat up straight in my chair, paying attention to every detail of the one who seemed to be the leader, and the guy right beside him. The more I stared, the more I realized I didn't know shit. The one thing I could see was that these guys were way older than me.

I took a picture of the freeze-frame and sent a message to both my brother and father with the picture attached, asking if either of them recognized either of these guys. Raydon texted back immediately, letting me know that he didn't, and a few minutes later, my father said the same.

I took a deep breath, exhaling slowly. I closed my eyes for a split second before opening them again, shutting my computer down. All the information for the business looked good, so there was no need to be here today. That's what my employees were for.

"A'ight, Angel. I'm out. Make sure these niggas do their jobs, and call me if you need me."

"OK, Reeno," Angel replied.

I pushed my way out the door and hopped into my Range that was parked right outside the door. I needed to ride past the now vacant house off Boswell Rd that had gotten robbed. A nigga was fucked up about my people who just went missing from the house; Vernon, Latrell, and Warren. I was responsible for every last one of my workers. The fact that three were missing, didn't sit well with me. I dropped the ball on this shit.

******

I pushed all the crazy shit that was going on to the side, knowing I was taking Eden out later on. Out of all the things going wrong in my life, she needed to be the one thing going right.

"Good evening, Reeno, my man."

Jameson, one of the building's security guards, greeted me as I walked past the security desk of my apartment building. I nodded at a few more people who spoke to me while they sat in the lobby.

"Good evening. How was your day, Jameson?"

"It's been great thus far. Thanks for asking."

I nodded, continuing to the elevator, headed up to my place. Once inside, I hurriedly undressed to shower so that I could get dressed and be on time picking Eden up.

I decided to drive my burnt orange Bentley Flying Spur. I had this shit hooked up with wood grain interior, black twenty-two-inch rims, and dark tinted windows. This Bentley was my favorite car to floss.

I pulled up to Destiny's house and parked my shit. I didn't get all the way out of the car before this loud mouth hoe started talking to me.

"Damn, nigga. You looking good. What's up?"

I glanced her way and frowned. Not only was her mouth foul and unattractive, but her face was too.

"With a face like that, sweetheart, you shouldn't have such a foul mouth."

Her bottom lip dropped to the concrete before she recovered and responded with, "Fuck you, nigga. You not all that anyway."

"Your panties say otherwise, hoe."

I turned around and knocked on Destiny's door.

"Hey, Reeno."

Destiny frowned at me. She peeked behind my back when she heard yelling and cursing.

"She talking to you, Reeno?"

"Yeah, her thirsty ass mad that I wouldn't give her no play. She saw money pull up and was trying to get her share."

"Yeah, her hoe ass tried to talk to Raydon before, and you know I shut that down. But Eden will be down here in a little bit."

Destiny opened the door wider so that I could enter her home. Five minutes later, I heard the clicking of heels coming down the stairs. I looked up just in time to see Eden's sexy ass. My posture stiffened as I shook my head, and my lips parted slightly. Everything inside a nigga went blank as I admired her in the sexy burgundy dress she had on, shit was crazy. We were matching and didn't even plan this shit.

"My, my, my, woman. Damn." I held out my hand for her to grab as she stepped off the last step.

"Aww, y'all match; isn't that cute." Destiny walked past us, headed to her room.

"Shut up, Destiny." Eden punched her in the back.

"You look great." I admired her as she spun around, giving me a view of her petite, yet round ass.

"You look quite debonair yourself." I noticed her rake her eyes over me from head to toe.

Of course, a nigga was suave in my black tailored pants with a black button-up and burgundy bow tie. My diamonds were shining in my ear and cufflinks, not to mention the diamonds on my bottom teeth.

"Let's get out of here before we not make it anywhere." My eyes moved over her body again before grabbing her hand and heading outside to let her in my car. I ignored ol' girl's dirty stares from across the street. She may want to get her shit together 'cause this isn't what she wants.

The drive over to the restaurant was awkward as fuck. We kept glancing at each other, giving little smirks and shit. Some ol' school girl shit. Every now and then we would say something to one another, questioning each other about our life. Other than that, it was quiet.

I pulled up to McCormick & Schmick's near South Park Mall. I handed my keys to the Valet as Eden latched on to my arm and we began walking into the restaurant. As soon as we entered, the hostess greeted me by name as most places did.

"Good evening, Ms. Lady."

"Mr. Brooks, your table is ready. Right this way."

I placed my hand possessively at the small of Eden's back as we followed the hostess. The murmurs of the people became distant once the hostess pushed open the double doors to a private area. It was a single table in the middle of the room that was decorated with a few candles and a bucket with champagne on ice.

The lights were dimly lit, and the smells from the mixture of foods had my stomach growling.

"Oh my god. You did all of this for me? We could have eaten with everyone else."

"I need you all to myself, beautiful. So I can think straight."

I was really trying this being respectful thing with Eden. I could definitely see that she was worth it. I turned to the hostess who was still standing there. For what, I didn't know. But I let her know that I had it from here. I lifted the bottle of Armand de Brignac Brut Gold, otherwise known as Ace of Spades, and poured two glasses of it.

We both took a few sips of the wine before the waiter knocked on the door and entered the small room once I said it was OK. He sat the plate of calamari that I requested when I made the reservation on the table.

"I ordered for us. I hope that's OK."

Eden only nodded her head with a wide smile on her face. Our conversation flowed effortlessly. I could see this between us going somewhere.

"How was your interview?"

"I think it went great. I had an interview at two different High Schools so far. Hopefully, one of them will contact me back soon."

"I'm sure they will."

I watched her sip on her Ace after chewing her calamari. Something told me to ask her if she knew what she was eating. She was popping them in her mouth like they were the best thing.

"Is it good?"

"Yes, these little things taste so good. I've never had them before."

I placed my hands on the table and smiled before I said, "That squid taste good, don't it?"

"What?"

She stopped eating and spit what she had in her mouth into a napkin.

"You mean to tell me you got me eating squid. Oh my Goooooood."

I laughed as she guzzled down the water that was also on the table. I was laughing so hard that my stomach hurt.

"I'm sorry, baby, but this shit is funny."

"It is not."

I turned my head when the waiter stepped back in with our entrées. I ordered her the south-west grilled salmon, shrimp, sautéed spinach with onions, and a loaded baked potato, and I had steak, instead of the salmon. Once she calmed down from eating squid, she was able to appreciate the meal.

I was really feeling the vibe between the two of us. That steak was good as fuck, and I could tell her food was good by the way she killed it. We spent our time in between chewing, asking each other questions. I could tell this shit was going to be the start of something great. As long as I remembered that she was not like the other women that had been around.

"I have to say, I am kind of upset this date is about to end." Eden let me know as we took our last bite of the cheesecake we shared.

"You know it doesn't have to. You can come chill at my house. Do you have anything to do in the morning?"

"No, I don't, but are you sure? I don't want to intrude on you."

"Baby girl, you won't ever interfere with anything I have to do. I asked because I want you there."

"OK then."

A nigga was glad she agreed.

I pushed my chair back and stood up, walking to the side of the table. I reached for her hand and kissed the back of it as she stood. I reached in my pocket, peeled off two-hundred dollars, and left it on the table. Eden giggled as she took a drunken step toward me.

"Girl, calm down. Let's go, beautiful." I grabbed her hand and we headed to my house.

Something felt off as soon as I reached for Eden to get out of the car. She was so happy, and I hated to ruin her fun. My eyes diverted in all directions, and that's when I saw someone dressed in all black ducked down between two cars to my right. He was easy to find, it was like he was hiding from other patrons, just not from me.

My right hand crossed over and under my jacket. That's when I felt Eden tense up and hold on to the back of my jacket. She saw my gun and opened her mouth to say something, but I cut her off, having to think fast.

"You see that door up ahead? Slip those shoes off right now, and when I say go, run inside and tell the guy at the desk to let you up to my apartment."

I began trying to be as normal as I could. I didn't want to alert whoever it was that I knew they were there. Eden did as I asked and slipped her shoes off quickly. I continued with my instructions.

"Tell him that it's an issue outside, and he will know what to do. His name is Jameson; now go."

I could see on her pretty little face that she was both scared and confused, but when I said go, she ran for her life as I covered her all the way to the door, and I started blastin' on that fool. I stood up, walking toward the guy, letting off shot after shot. I ducked behind a car to duck his shots. When I didn't hear any more bullets, I popped up, and let off six quick shots.

Things were quiet for a moment until I heard tires screeching. I already knew it was my brother because those were Jameson's instructions, just in case something happened. My hand tightened on the trigger as I backed up toward my brother once he stepped out of the car.

"What's up, bruh?"

"Man, I need you to take care of this, and then come up and we'll talk. Eden was with me, and I know she is losing her mind, bro."

"Where is she?" Raydon turned around to look for her, but I explained where she was.

"I made sure she got inside, and she told Jameson to let her up and call you. But do that for me please."

Of course, my brother was going to hold me down. He gave me a hug and then got to work as I ran toward the glass double doors.

"Hurry to your friend. She is crying and upset," Jameson let me know.

"Thanks for that. My brother is taking care of everything. He will be in here in a sec." With that said, I got on the elevator.

Eden

My airways seemed restricted as I ran for my life with bullets flying past me. I had never been in anything like that in my entire life. The guy at the desk, who I'm guessing was Jameson, seemed as if he already knew something was wrong. He sprang into action without me really having to say anything, except for him to let me up to Reeno's place.

My palms were sweaty, and I kept wiping them on my dress. I heard more gunshots, which wasn't helping me at all. I was now worried about Reeno and what was happening with him. Jameson hurriedly escorted me to the elevator and pressed the code that led to Reeno's place before walking away.

I stepped off of the elevator once it stopped, and the door opened, then I went straight to the couch. This was too much. I was actually having a good time with this man, and now this. Could I really be the type of woman behind a man that has no problem killing someone? Because I'm sure that was what was happening right now.

I looked toward the elevator when I heard it open. I watched Reeno loosen his tie and unbutton the top of his shirt to get more comfortable. I stood and ran toward him while wiping my tearstained face. My arms circled his neck as I stated, "I was so worried."

He held me, rubbing my back while kissing my cheek, encouraging me to calm down.

"I got you, Eden. I won't let anything happen to you, OK?"

I pulled away, nodding my head as he wiped the tears from my face.

"I was so scared." I reached up to help him remove his jacket, which afterward, he finished unbuttoning his shirt and removed it as well.

"I hate you had to see that part of me. Shit, we just met, and this happens," Reeno expressed.

Reeno led me over to the couch and sat down before pulling me onto his lap. Being in his arms felt good; too good. This was something I could definitely get used to. He was whispering in my ear, letting me know that this would never happen again.

We both looked up when we heard the elevator. My brother Raydon stepped off. Raydon first asked if I was doing OK, then he gave me a hug.

"Y'all good?" He looked between the two of us.

"We're both fine, so I'm good."

"I need to talk to him for a minute. My room is the first one on the left. Whatever you need, if you want to take a shower, it's in there." Reeno pointed to his brother and then down the hallway toward his room.

I stood and made my way down the hallway to the room he said was his. I stripped down, needing this damn shower. I didn't know where we would go from here, but I wasn't ready to give up just yet.

Chapter 8

Destiny

"As you can see, this home is perfect. It's exactly what you asked for, Mr. Mason. It has every detail that you requested, from having an open floor plan downstairs, a loft upstairs, and a jacuzzi tub in the master suite. You also have a gigantic back yard for your gatherings you love to have." I smiled as I spoke to my current client that I was showing a house to.

I was really excited about showing this particular home. It was in the Ballantyne area and was on the market for $450,000. The commission on this baby was going to be off the chain.

"Please, call me Mace."

The handsome stranger corrected as he attacked my body with his eyes before licking his dark lips, looking as if he smoked Black and Milds.

"But you're right, Ms. Destiny. It is perfect. How soon can you get the paperwork ready, shorty?"

"No more than three days," I told him as we made our way to the front door.

"Sounds good, baby. Now that business is out of the way..." Mace let his words linger for a minute.

I stopped, turning around, wondering what he meant by that statement. My brow was raised as I waited for him to finish.

"I want to get to know you." He walked up on me. I took a step back as I was engulfed by his cologne. I took the time to look him over, and he was fine as fuck. He didn't compare to Raydon though.

"I got a man, baby, and I don't date my clients."

"Good thing this will be a quick sell," Mace whispered in my ear.

This dude needed to step back. He was so close to me that I thought we were about to kiss or something. I took a step back, and he took a step forward. Damn, this man was fine as hell. I didn't mix business with pleasure, but he may have been worth it. It's not like me and Raydon were on the same page right now. I was really thinking about entertaining this guy.

He took another step toward me. This time we were damn near touching. My breathing quickened, and my eyes blinked rapidly, causing him to smirk. This dude had balls. The next thing I knew, his hands were on my waist, pulling me forward.

"So what's up, ma. Can I get your number or what?"

"It's on the paperwork," I whispered.

"Nah, I want it now, and I want your personal line, not your business line. Don't play me, ma."

How could I say no to this man? He was definitely slick with it. I grabbed his phone that he pulled from his pocket and entered my number. When I gave it back, he called my phone so that I would also have his number.

"I will be calling you soon for our first date. And you hit me when you have those papers together." Mace stepped around me and walked out the front door.

My lungs expanded as I let go of the breath I was holding. I waited a few minutes before leaving, giving him time to leave. I then locked up the house and left to finish out my day.

******

The house was quiet when I walked inside my home. Checking the time, I wondered where Eden could be. She said she would be home this evening, but I don't see any signs of her. I knew Eden said she would be here, but maybe she changed her mind. I locked up the house, set my alarm, and headed upstairs.

I stopped in my tracks when I saw Eden on the couch staring straight ahead. I knew something was wrong, and I was going to find out what it was. I flipped the light switch on the wall to turn the ceiling lights on. I then set my purse and keys down on the coffee table before sitting next to Eden.

"Honey, what's wrong?" I reached for Eden's hand and held it in my own.

She turned her head toward me and asked, "Is this how it's going to be? Is this what it's like talking to Reeno and Raydon?"

"What do you mean? What happened?" I inquired, thinking that something terrible must have happened for her to be feeling this way. I was praying that it didn't have anything to do with another woman.

Eden shook her head from left to right as she ran down the story for me of what happened last night.

"It was terrible, Des, but one thing I can't take from him is that he protected me before he did anything else. How can I really be mad at that? Well, I'm not really mad, but terrified that this is only the beginning."

"Truthfully, E, I have never experienced anything like that. I hate that you did. It seems as if you were his priority though, which is a good thing." I attempted to lighten the mood a little bit.

"Yeah, you are right. It was just so scary though. I felt something was wrong before anything happened. I'm trying my best to get the shit out of my head." Eden placed her feet on the ground and stood up to stretch.

"How about we go to the mall?" I asked.

"Yeah, we can do that. I need to buy new clothes for work anyway." Eden smiled.

"OMG! You got the job?"

"Yes, the lady sent me an unofficial email this morning that basically means I got it. I just have to wait to get a start date. You know teachers start a little in advance.

"That's great, cuzo."

"But just take it slow with Reeno. I'm glad you're OK though, boo." I hugged her.

"I need to take a quick shower. I will meet you back down here in a few."

******

We had a few bags in our hands as we strolled through the mall. There weren't many people here this evening. I noticed Eden finally enjoying herself, which was what I wanted.

"So, how are things with you and Raydon?"

Eden asked as we sat down with our Chick-fil-a meals. I didn't say anything at first. For real, I didn't want to talk about him, but I knew she wouldn't let it go.

"I had to give his ass an ultimatum. I really like him, maybe even love him, Eden, but he acts like he can't do anything with me besides fuck. Since you have been here, this is the most we've went out. If he can't give me more, then I'm going to show his ass that he isn't the only nigga who I can get."

"Be careful with that shit, cuz. I can already tell he is crazy over you. I think he wants to give you more, but he wants his cake and eat it too. You better check these hoes."

"That's the thing, I never see him with anyone, and no one approaches me." I ate the last of my waffle fries before cleaning my spot.

"I like y'all together. Just see how it plays out."

"I feel you."

Chapter 9

Beast

I walked down the squeaky steps to check on these lame ass niggas that were working for Reeno. As soon as I hit the bottom step, I saw Vernon, Warren, and Latrell working hard to cut up that product I stole from those bitch ass niggas.

This was the only way that I could put them to work. I knew I couldn't leave them out on the streets. They would be seen, if not by Reeno and Raydon, then by someone on their team would.

The crazy thing about this situation was that this shit didn't even start with them, but they included themselves when they killed my cousin. My cousin was only here because of what Bear did to my father. It's too bad that his sons would have to pay for his mistake, along with him.

"I'm glad you niggas decided to cooperate." I snickered.

"I didn't want to come down here and beat anyone's ass."

No one said anything, and I'm glad they didn't. Their asses were probably plotting on how to get out of here, but too bad there wasn't a way.

"I need y'all to do something for me. Be ready in a few days. You're going to his other spot." The mugs on Vernon, Warren, and Latrell's faces put a smile on mine.

Chapter 10

Reeno

I needed to go speak with my father. It was Friday night, and I knew I could catch him at the club. I pulled up beside the dumpster in the back alley, parking my car. I got out, looking dapper as always, chillin' in a pair of jeans and a Polo with a pair of Air Max Flyknits.

I entered the establishment through the back door, heading straight to my father's office. I didn't want to get distracted, which is why I didn't go through the front for A'Myracle to see me.

As I was closer to my father's office, I stopped in my tracks when I heard the elevation of his voice. My father didn't raise his voice often. This was an indication that someone really pissed him off. I normally wouldn't eavesdrop, but the words he was saying had my ass hot.

"His ass shouldn't even be out of prison. If he is the one causing problems for my boys, then I need to know now."

I couldn't hear what the other person was saying, of course. But I could tell Stanford wasn't happy about the shit. This shit made me think that he knew more about those niggas being after us than he led on. I still hadn't found my other men, leading me to believe they were dead.

I pushed his office door open, not being able to stand there any longer. I grimaced at my father through narrowed eyes, questioning him before he even opened his mouth.

"Aye, let me call you back later. My son just walked in... yes, OK... bye." Stanford finally hung up the phone.

He glanced up at me, waiting to see how much of his conversation I heard.

"What was that about? Who shouldn't be out of prison? And if you had an issue with someone, why not tell us?"

"Son, don't read into this too much. I've been in this game much longer than you." Stanford stood to his feet, which caused me to stand as well.

"Bullshit, Pop. I believe you know what's going on."

"Don't raise your fucking voice at me. I'm still your father." Stanford's fist hit the wood on his desk.

"If and when I feel the need to give you information, I will. Until then, get the fuck out of my office."

I frowned, looking back at this nigga. Since when did he keep secrets? This led me to believe that my instincts were right. I was going to back up for now, but I would definitely be revisiting this shit. In the meantime, I pulled out my phone and sent a text to David, informing him to put a word out. Ten thousand dollars for each one of his soldiers who were found.

Leaving my father's office, I walked right next door to my own. Yes, this was my father's place, but my brother and I had a hand in it too. I stopped in my tracks, seeing A'Myracle spread eagle on my large desk, naked as the day she was born. If this was another time, I probably would have fucked the shit out of her ass, but I wasn't interested right now. I didn't know if it was because of this shit with my father, or because Eden was invading my brain.

I stared at her ass for a minute before walking toward her. I spotted her clothes on the floor and picked them up, saying, "Get dressed," as I threw them at her.

The smile she held a second ago dropped. Her mouth opened and shut a few times, probably from the shock of me talking to her this way. I had never turned her ass down. Instead of her ass listening, she jumped down from my desk and walked seductively toward me. Her hips swaying each time her foot hit the ground.

"You know you want to fuck me, Reeno. You always do." She grabbed my pants, noticing that I wasn't even aroused.

I was about to say something as I knocked her hand away, but my phone vibrated in my pocket. Once realizing that it was Eden, I stood and walked over to the window that overlooked the club.

"What's up, baby?"

"I want to see you," Eden answered.

"Oh, really? I can make that happen," I responded.

"Can I come to your place?" Eden asked.

"Yes, be on the way. If you get there before me, have Jameson let you up. I will give him the heads up." I let her know before we ended the conversation.

"Really, nigga. I'm standing here ass naked, and you taking a call from another bitch?" A'Myracle's fists were clenched like she wanted to punch me.

"I bet you better get your ass out my face. I don't owe you a got damn thing, A'Myracle. Don't start this. You have been good. It's best you not get on my bad side." With that being said, I left out of my office with the door wide open. I didn't give a damn if anyone saw her ass naked or not.

******

"Hello, Mr. Brooks. I let Ms. Eden up as you requested," Jameson greeted.

"Appreciate it." I bypassed Jameson and headed toward the elevator. When I walked off into my place, Eden was standing in front of the large windows, taking in the view of the city. She turned around to greet me when I was close to her.

"Hey." She smiled up at me.

"What's good."

"This view is amazing. I guess I didn't notice it last week with everything that happened." She shook her head.

I didn't say anything; I just positioned myself behind her, grabbing her waist. I kissed her neck a few times before expressing how sorry I was for having her in that predicament. She turned around and wrapped her arms around my neck. She leaned in and pecked me on my lips.

I admired her when she pulled back. Eden was a fucking masterpiece, and I wouldn't let her slip away. They say everyone has that one person who is for them, and I believe that Eden was that one. I moved a piece of hair that had fallen in her face, and said, "Listen, let's not talk about that shit anymore." I nuzzled my face against her neck. This girl smelled so damn good.

"But we have to…" Eden pulled away and walked over to the couch to sit down before continuing. "If I'm going to continue whatever this is…" Her finger pointed between the two of us as she finished. "I need to know more about you, about this life you live, so if there is a next time, I will be prepared instead of scared."

I smiled at her little ass wanting that gangsta to come out of her.

"So you do want to deal with me. I was getting kind of fearful since I haven't heard from you since that night." My right hand scratched the top of my head while I shook it from side to side; I really thought she was done.

"I mean, you have a wonderful spirit about you. No matter what you're into, I know you are a good man." Eden had a nigga cheesing like hell.

"In all honesty, I usually don't tell my business like that, but I trust your little ass. I'm the plug baby. I live a complicated life. My father passed his empire down to my brother and me. We haven't had issues since we began, because we treat everyone like family. We knew that it was a possibility of someone having issues, but we are prepared. As soon as we use our resources to find out who it is, we will handle the situation accordingly. But what I can say is, I protect the ones I care about. If anyone messes with you, they have to deal with me. You are attached to me now, baby girl; ain't no leaving." My thumb and index finger went to my beard as I waited for her to respond.

I was getting scared for a minute. Maybe I went too hard on her. Her eyes were on my floors before she looked up, eased that damn beautiful smile on her face, and said, "I guess you told me." We both laughed.

I stood and informed her that I needed to shower and that she could make herself comfortable. I walked to my bathroom and turned the water on while I undressed. I stepped into the shower and lathered my body before standing under the water to rinse it off.

I felt a whiff of cool air hit my body, causing me to turn around. *Got damn,* I thought to myself, licking my lips as I admired this amazing sculpture in front of me. Eden was skinny, but she had enough, and I loved it. I could throw her little ass around however I wanted. I reached out for her hand, helping her step over the edge of the tub.

Once she was inside, her eyes raked over my body, stiffening at the sight of my long and thick semi-hard dick. I stroked her arms sensually, backing her to the wet wall in my large shower, calming her down. My heart thundered in my chest, wondering if she was going to let me feel the heaven between her thighs. I bent down and kissed her from her lips, down to her breasts. Her head fell back as I flicked my tongue over her dark, hardened nipple.

"Mmmm." The moan that slipped from her lips had my dick stretching by the inch.

In one motion, I placed my hands on her hips and lifted her with her back against the wall, and pussy in my face. Her legs wrapped around my neck as she screamed out in ecstasy.

I slurped and blew on her pussy while holding her up with one hand and toyed with her clit with the other hand. Her small body trembled as she sprayed me with her juices. I gently eased her down, licking her neck until she came down from her high. I quickly washed her before turning the water off. I stepped out of the shower and helped her out before leading her to the bedroom.

I laid her flat on her back, hovering over her and asked, "Is this what you really want? I know I said if you in, you're in, but I'm man enough to give you one more out." I leaned down, slipping my tongue into her mouth, swirling it around, causing her to do the same. She moaned in my mouth as her small hand went between us. Without a word, she grabbed my dick and guided it into her warm, inviting pussy. She hissed as my thickness invaded her private spot. I could see she was having trouble accepting my length, so I took over. I entered her and pulled out a couple of times, going in deeper each time I plunged in her shit.

"Damn, girl."

I had to start off slow from fear that a nigga was going to bust quick. I lifted both of her legs to gain better access. At that point, I showed no mercy. I wanted her to know exactly what she was dealing with. The curve of my dick was hittin' her spot every time I dug deep. I knew because she yelped almost every time. Her shit was getting juicer by the minute. I pulled out and lifted her, walking a few steps to the dresser, placing her on top. I bent down and took one big lick of her pussy.

I lifted one of her legs, planting her foot on top of it before entering her again. I held her waist, giving her those death strokes.

"Oh yes, baby. Fuck me."

"I know you like this shit, girl. Ain't no turning back now, baby. No other nigga better not touch my pussy. Do you hear me?"

It took her time to get herself under control before she screamed 'yes' at the top of her lungs. Again, her body was shaking, and I was right behind her, sounding like a big ass bear. I had to laugh at myself as I pulled out as cum shot out onto the floor. The way I sounded, you would have thought I hadn't had pussy in years.

Raydon

Destiny had been heavy on my mind. Even though we had sex after she gave me that bitch ass ultimatum, we still didn't end that night on good terms. She wanted a nigga to do too much. I did have heavy feelings for the girl, but damn, I wanted to make sure I was going to treat her right and leave these hoes alone when the time came. A nigga's heart was in the right place. Hopefully, she would realize that.

I picked up my phone, not being able to take it any longer. I dialed her number twice, both times getting the same results; her voicemail. I knew one thing, her ass better not be with another nigga doing some shit she knew I wouldn't approve of.

Not being able to get in contact with Destiny had me doing something I probably shouldn't have been doing; going to the damn club.

I walked into the club and bypassed everyone to get to my office. I sat at my desk, picking up the phone to call Steven, the club manager. I informed him that I was there and needed to speak to Tiffany. A few minutes later, she was walking into my office topless.

"What's up, Raydon? Steven said you called for me?"

She stood there with one hand on her hip, with her hip poked out.

"You know what it is, Tiff. I need a release."

She didn't ask any more questions, which is what I liked about her. Homegirl was on her knees in two-point-five seconds, releasing me from my sweats. She licked the length down to my balls, getting it wet the way I liked it. Next thing I knew, my fucking toes were curling in my slides. I grabbed a fist full of her hair to control her movements a little bit.

Her head bobbed as she moaned, giving me that vibration down my shaft. Her hand went to my balls as she squeezed them, gently pushing me there. Seconds later, I was shooting down her throat. I smacked her ass as she stood and turned around.

"Where you think you going, girl?"

"You said you needed a release, so I figured was done."

"Nah, bend that ass over my desk. I'm not finished." I removed a condom from my wallet and rolled it down my dick.

I could tell she was excited as fuck. This was the first time I'd ever asked her to fuck. Whenever we got together, she only sucked my dick.

"I knew you always wanted a taste of this pussy," she sexily stated.

"Shut your ass up, and bend over before I change my damn mind." I let her ass know, and of course, she shut the fuck up and bent her ass over.

I wanted this to be quick, but I wasn't a selfish lover. I fucked her until it looked like her ass was having an out-of-body experience before I pulled out and released inside the condom. Oh, what you thought, just because I had a condom on I was going to nut inside this hoe? Not a damn chance. A nigga didn't trust these hoes.

"A'ight, go wash and get back to work."

"That's it? Just fuck me, and I have to go back to work?"

See, this is exactly why I didn't like sticking my dick anywhere. I knew this was going to be a damn mistake. She done got the dick, and now she thought she had privileges. Let me straighten this shit right now.

"What you thought? You get dick from one of the bosses and then move up in the world? Nah, boo, shit doesn't work like that. Get your ass in the bathroom before my father finds out you're fraternizing." I sat down in my chair, waiting on her to freshen up so that I could use my bathroom.

Soon after I left the club, I was feeling kind of bad how I treated Tiffany, but oh, well. I glanced down at my phone and frowned when I didn't see a returned call from Destiny. This girl was going to make me choke her out.

Putting my truck in drive, I pulled off and headed back to Destiny's house.

"Hello." I picked up my phone when it rang, hoping that it was her, but it was my brother instead.

"What's up, Raydon?"

"What's going on?"

"Man, I think your pops is hiding something," Reeno expressed.

"Nigga, that's your daddy too, but why do you think that?" I asked.

"Well, I walked in on him saying some shit about somebody not supposed to be out of prison yet. When I stepped into his office, he hurriedly got off the phone. When I asked him about it, he got all defensive. The shit sounded fucked up. Only thing I could think is that he has an idea about who hit our spot," he informed me.

"Damn, I hope he is not keeping no shit from us."

I didn't think our father would do any shit like that, but these days, you never know.

"He told me he would say something if he finds out anything worth telling," Reeno continued.

"Well, let's just play it by ear. You know pops wouldn't do anything to get us hurt. He would suit up for us," I responded as I pulled onto Destiny's street.

"Yeah, you are right. But let me get off this phone, Eden is sleeping."

"Let me find out, nigga. You got her at your house. I know it's real, Reeno."

"Shut your ass up. I'll holla, nigga." Reeno hung up and I laughed.

My joyful moment ended when I didn't see Destiny's car. I parked my ass down the street; she was going to have a rude awakening when her ass got home.

******

"I had a great time tonight. I normally don't go out with my clients, but I'm glad I did," I heard Destiny say as I sat at the kitchen table.

"I'm glad you answered my call, beautiful. You go ahead and get some sleep. You can call me tomorrow."

I heard a nigga say, and I wasn't too pleased about the shit. I had been waiting on her for the past three hours. I broke in when she was taking too long. I needed to get this shit handled fast.

Destiny walked into the kitchen, not even realizing that I was there at first. She walked in and opened the refrigerator door, and that's when I stood up and asked, "Where the fuck you been?"

"Ahhhh!" She screamed as the water bottle she had just grabbed fell to the floor.

She flicked the light switch on and squealed, "What the fuck are you doing in my house?"

I tilted my head, stood up, and walked toward her, asking, "No, the question is, where the fuck you been with that nigga? Better yet, who is that nigga?" I spoke coolly.

"None of your business. I gave you the opportunity to pick me, and you didn't. Just because we had sex, doesn't mean shit." She picked up her things and headed for the stairs.

I followed after her, saying, "Destiny, I told your ass not to fuck with me."

"And I told your ass to leave me alone, Raydon. What don't you get?"

Her voice cracked, indicating that she was on the verge of crying. I didn't want her ass crying, but she wasn't about to be parading around town with another nigga either. She threw her shoes in the corner before walking toward the bed. I grabbed her arm, spinning her around and using my pointer to lift her chin.

"Baby, I do want you. I promise I do." I leaned in to kiss her, but she reached back and smacked my ass before stepping back.

"You've got some nerve. Coming up in here talking about you want me, but you smell like another bitch. Get the fuck out, Raydon." With her small fist, Destiny punched me in the chest, and she was beginning to piss me off.

"I don't smell like another bitch, Destiny. I've been at the club."

"And which one of those hoes you fuck? You are not slick, nigga. I see how some of them look when we are in there together.

Get the fuck out of my house, and don't hit me up until you are serious."

"Destiny?"

"Get the fuck out!" She screamed in my face before shutting herself in her bathroom.

"Come on, Des. She only gave me head, and that's only because you wasn't answering. And don't think you slick either. I'm going to find out who that nigga was. And then it's lights out for his ass." I stood there for a minute, realizing that she wasn't going to answer me. I decided to go ahead and leave for now, but you better believe, I would have my eyes on her ass.

Chapter 11

Eden

My eyes fluttered before fully opening. A smile graced my face, remembering last night's activities. Reeno had my body feeling as if I was in another world; one with clear water and pretty butterflies landing in my hair. I haven't felt this way in... well, I haven't ever felt this way in my twenty-three years of life. Shoot, if I had to be down for him, that's what I would do. He had my head so gone that I was willing to learn how to shoot a gun if I had to. Imagine that.

I sat up, stretching my body while yawning. Reeno wasn't in the bed, but I heard the shower running and decided to join him. I was sure he wouldn't mind starting the day like we finished last night.

I stepped into the shower, walking right up to him and circling his waist with my arms. He dipped his head and tongued me down nastily. There were no words spoken as he lifted me by my ass and placed himself at my opening before pushing himself into me.

He was sure to make me cum several times before washing me, followed by himself. Afterward, we were both dressed.

"Are you going to hang with me today, Ms. Eden?" He walked up on me, circling his arms around my thin waist.

"Is that an invitation?" I used my hand to bring his face forward for a kiss.

After pecking him a few times, he picked me up, placing me on the dresser and responded, "It sure is, baby." He waited on me to answer while groping my thighs.

"In that case, I'd love to."

"OK, I'm going to take you to get something to eat."

******

Reeno pulled up to Terrace Café, parking his Matte Gray Porsche right out front. He stepped out of the car, looking as good as ever, and rounded the car to get me. He held my hand the whole way, and I was loving the attention.

The décor of the restaurant was beautiful. There was a trendy chalkboard that listed specials for the day sitting right up front. I was about to take a seat, considering there were others waiting, but I heard the waitress tell us to follow them. I shrugged my shoulders and rolled with it.

Of course, we were led to a private area. Well, it wasn't a private room, it was just on the other side of the building where clearly, wasn't nobody being seated.

"This is a nice place," I said as I sat down.

"The food is really good too; they have red velvet waffles."

"I am definitely going to order that." I giggled.

Everything was going well after we ordered until someone stopped beside our table with a frown on her face. This girl looked mad as hell that Reeno was here with someone else. I didn't give a damn though. As long as she didn't say shit to me, Reeno could handle his own business.

Reeno was annoyed. I watched him as he sighed heavily, narrowing his eyes at her. His masculine jaw clenched as he gawked at her, asking what she wanted without opening his mouth.

"I see why you haven't been answering my phone calls."

This girl stood there with a whole attitude, not even caring that I was sitting there. Reeno didn't reply right away. He actually pulled his phone from his pocket and sent a text before he answered, "If I haven't been answering your calls, then that should tell you something, that I don't want to talk to your ass. I'll holla at you later. As you can see, I'm in the presence of a queen."

I blushed at him calling me that in front of this hoe. I smiled as I glanced up at her eyeing me. I wasn't with the drama, but I also didn't take no shit from anybody. As long as her hands stayed to herself, then I'm straight.

"Hmm, her skinny ass couldn't hold a light to me on her best day, and clearly this isn't her best day."

I knew this girl was only trying to get me riled up, so of course, I sat there looking pretty and said, "Nice try. A queen such as myself will never let a hoe like you get me out of character. Why don't you run along, sweetie? It's obvious that he has been sending you a hint. I'm here now. No need for you to be around." I nonchalantly picked up my Arnold Palmer, taking a sip of it before sitting up straight in my chair, placing my folded hands on the table. My eyes stayed on this hoe, daring her to take a swing.

Reeno was amused; he chuckled and added, "Get the fuck from my table. The queen has spoken. And if you start something, I will cut your titty off."

I grabbed my breasts, thinking about him doing that shit for real. I hated it for her.

"Fuck you, Reeno." She turned on her heels and stormed away.

Reeno's hand slid down his face while saying, "I'm sorry baby. I don't like that shit, and I know you don't either. Let's finish our breakfast and enjoy our day. Forget about the ones who aren't wanted."

With that said, the two of us enjoyed breakfast without any more issues. The more I got to know Reeno, the more I was really feeling this dude.

******

I walked through the front door of Destiny's home. I had a little pep in my step after spending last night and part of today with Reeno. The first thing I did was go into my room so that I could take a shower and put something on more comfortable. I didn't have plans on going anywhere else today. It was mid-June, so school would be starting in about two months. I needed to start working on lesson plans. I had so much in store for my students that I couldn't wait.

The shower was refreshing, but nothing compared to the beating Reeno put on my body. I was counting down the time until I saw him again

"Damn, it's like that?" Destiny stopped in front of my room.

I was dancing to some Reggaetón song that was playing through my Tidal app.

"Huh?"

"Girl, don't *huh* me. You over here cheesing and dancing around your room. Plus, you didn't come home last night, Ms. fast ass." Destiny's eyebrows rose and fell rapidly as she laughed.

Although she was laughing, I saw that her eyes were puffy. I turned my music off and moved across the carpet toward her. I placed my hand on her shoulder and asked, "What's going on?"

Destiny stared at me for a minute before her lip trembled, and her face flushed red. She used the back of her hand to wipe her tears away.

"Raydon got me fucked up, Eden. He had the nerve to come over last night, break in my house, and be waiting on me when my date dropped me off. I don't know how he knew but..."

"Wait, you had a date last night? With who? Now you knew that nigga was going to act up." I was shocked by her revelation.

"I know, but it was friendly. A guy I sold a house to. It was innocent on my end. Although baby is fine as fuck. I think I made a mistake. But that's not the kicker. Raydon smelled as if he came from fucking another bitch. He had the nerve to admit that she only sucked his dick. That shit was so disrespectful." Destiny began to descend the stairs with me on her heels.

"So what exactly are you two trying to do? If y'all want to talk to other people, then do that." I sat on the couch, patting the seat next to me for Destiny to sit down.

"You know I want to be with him, but he is the one who doesn't know what he wants. I don't know what to do, but waiting isn't something I am interested in." Destiny's head fell back onto her red leather couch.

"You guys will figure it out. If it's meant to be, then it will be."

"You're right. Now don't think you are off the hook, you gave Reeno some cootie, didn't you?" Destiny asked.

"Eew you make it sound so nasty." I blushed.

"I knew it; he had your ass in there all happy and shit. I know he fucked the shit out of you, girl. If he is anything like his brother."

"Oh my god, stop with your nosy ass." I giggled, hitting her on her arm. I was just glad that she wasn't crying anymore.

After talking about those crazy ass Brooks brothers, we decided to have a girl's night in. Destiny grabbed the popcorn, and I retrieved the snacks. Of course, we had a bottle or two of wine on deck. I guess I wouldn't be formulating a lesson plan today.

Chapter 12

Warren

A couple of days later

I wiped my forehead as I listened to the bullshit that Beast was talking about. I saw Vernon's eyebrows rise, probably thinking the same thing that I was. There was no way that we were going to get away with what he was asking us to do.

"This shit will never work," I heard Latrell say from the other side of the table.

The next thing I knew, Latrell's brains were scattered on the wall behind him. I looked over at Beast, whose gun was still smoking. I couldn't believe this shit. He shot my nigga for voicing his opinion.

"The next person that questions me will cause all of you to get killed. You will do what the fuck I say. Now, here are some ski masks and gloves. I'm not that stupid to make you go in there with nothing over your face. If this dumb mothafucka..." He kicked Latrell's body before continuing, "would have listened, then he would be alive."

Vernon and I reached up and caught the items that were thrown at us. I wasn't at all excited about what this Beast nigga wanted us to do. However, I'd rather do this than to end up dead like my nigga. I closed my eyes for a second after glancing at Latrell's dead body.

Another man walked through the door, giving Beast dap. He was seeing if we were ready to go. Reluctantly, the two of us stood in our old dingy clothing that we'd been given to wear when we were finally allowed to bathe.

The ride was silent as Vernon and me were in our own thoughts. I couldn't believe that we had really got caught slippin' the way that we did when we were kidnapped. I had a good damn idea though. You see, Beast fucked up. No one knew these trailer park boys better than I did. This was in my territory. I just hoped I was recognized before shots rang out. These boys were crazy as fuck.

Pulling right outside of Lamplighter Village in front of the large church on the corner, the driver instructed us to go ahead and pull our mask down. We were then handed a .45 in our gloved hands before exiting the car. I led the way as we discussed prior to getting there. It was past midnight, and it wasn't anyone outside. The ones that were, were high doing their own thing, so they didn't pay any attention to three masked men walking through the trailer parks.

These trailers were old. The siding on them was dingy as if they hadn't been washed in years. Paper littered the ground from people not giving a damn what the place looked like. Clothing lines could be seen in the backyards with clothes hanging from them, almost touching the ground.

I located the first home I was looking for and pointed to Vernon and Beast's brother, who quickly ducked off, moving that way. Then I kept it moving to the space across the lot and a few spaces down.

Before knocking on the back door, I lifted my ski mask. You see, this was Zack and Chad's cousin. I was going to get word back to Reeno and Raydon tonight.

"George, we don't have much time." I walked in and ran down everything quickly. Next thing you know, I was running out of there with a duffle bag as George pretended to shoot at my ass.

Reeno

"The mobile homes? How in the fuck did they even know about that spot? That's why I picked the shit. Who would ever think that much money and product would be held up in a mobile home park?" I exploded as Zack relayed to me what his cousin relayed to him.

We were in a private room at Chill with Raydon and Stanford. This shit was getting out of hand. That was two spots. That was a lot of money and product. Whoever was responsible for this shit must pay with their life.

"Wait though, you haven't heard the best part," Zack interrupted.

"What could possibly be worse?" Raydon inquired.

"It was Warren and Vernon. Latrell is dead, according to Warren. He was shot because he didn't want to go along with what this Beast dude was telling them to do, which was rob y'all," Zack added.

"You mean to tell me our own team robbed us? Oh hell, nah."

"Nah, it's not like that. As soon as Warren got in there, he told my cousin what it was. He gave him the address of where they are being held." Zack held up a piece of paper for me to grab.

I glanced down at the piece of paper before handing it to my brother and father. I cracked my knuckles as I ground my teeth. I couldn't believe this shit, and when I looked up at my brother, then my father, I could see that the both of them knew why I was angry as fuck.

"Those mothafuckas have been under our noses this whole fucking time. This shit is crazy."

I sat my ass down in a chair and looked to my brother. He knew what I was saying, even though no words were coming out of my mouth. He read my thoughts. He knew I was ready to go straight to that warehouse and wreak havoc. However, his thoughts were to plan. I sighed looking over at my father. He was fidgeting in his seat.

"What's good, old man? Looks like you have something on your mind."

Stanford leaned back in his chair, crossing his arms over his chest. He squinted his eyes at me like I asked something I wasn't supposed too.

"No… no I'm good, son. Nothing is wrong with me."

I could tell he was lying, which prompted me to look at my brother with a raised brow. This made me think back to hearing Stanford on the phone. He was definitely keeping a secret. I could tell that now.

"So, what are y'all plans, you know we down for whatever you trying to do," Chad blurted while smoking his stinking ass cigarette. I hated those things, but to each his own.

My phone buzzed in my pocket. I reached for it and saw that it was a text from Eden.

Hey babe. What you getting into tonight.

I quickly texted back, *you if you want me to be.*

I guess I was cheesing a little too hard because I looked up to everybody staring at me.

"I don't want to hear shit." I chuckled, already knowing what they were thinking.

"I wasn't going to say shit, bruh." My brother said with his hands up in mock surrender.

"Well, I was. I know that look. Your mother did that for me for a while," my father added.

"Yeah, OK, back to the subject matter. Me and Raydon are going to go scope this place out tonight. Once we do, we will get with you two." I pointed to Zack and Chad. Everyone agreed to get back up once we saw what was going on.

As I was walking out of the building, A'Myracle's ass grabbed my arm. I really wasn't on this shit right now, but I was going to hear her out.

"What's up, girl?"

"I have to tell you something, Reeno."

"It has to wait, baby girl. Me and Raydon got shit to do. Holla at me tomorrow."

"But..." A'Myracle whined.

"No buts, that nigga waiting on my ass. Just hit me tomorrow," I told her, and then continued to walk in the direction that I was going.

I pulled up to the parking area at our warehouse off Davidson St. It's crazy that we could actually see their building from the roof of our warehouse. We needed binoculars to see it, but still. The point was, those niggas was too close for comfort.

"I still can't believe this, bro."

Raydon spoke as he walked behind me up the stairs, on the way to the roof. I had my black book bag that carried binoculars and whatever other items we may need. We were finally at the top of the roof, walking over to the East side of the building where we could see across to Beast's building.

"Who you tellin'? But did you see how pops was acting? He was staring at nothing like he was thinkin' hard about something. I'm telling you, it's something he's hiding."

"Yeah, I caught that, bro. I just hope he comes clean. I don't mind bustin' my guns. But at least let me know why I'm bustin' them shits."

"Right." I held my hand out and my brother slapped hands with me. I reached in my bag, handing my brother a pair of binoculars while I pulled out the other pair for myself. We spent a few hours watching and plotting. When we got up in there, they wouldn't know who hit they asses.

Stanford "Bear" Brooks

Beast... I thought to myself. I couldn't do anything but shake my head. I knew that man really well, although the last time I saw him, he was a young boy, had to be around eighteen. He was the son of my right hand when I was in the streets heavy. Me and Zell were niggas since middle school.

We were both all about money since a young age. We were both smart as fuck leading us both to get into Morehouse College. We were the hood niggas on campus. Everyone knew to come to us for their drug of choice. We were killing it to be so young. After graduating college, we went head first, quickly moving up the ladder of command until we were the plugs.

Everything went good for years until we got on the Feds radar. I had someone on the inside of course, but Zell didn't know it. The detective I was in cahoots with let me know that the force planned on showing up at the next drop to arrest us.

The only thing I could think about was my wife and kids. No one mattered to me at the moment, not even my nigga, Zell. Call me what you want, but you won't call me incarcerated or dead, which is what happened to Zell.

That evening, the summer of 1998, would forever be etched in my mind. I called up Zell earlier that day, telling him that my wife, Leena, wasn't feeling well, and I couldn't tag along. He assured me that it was OK, and that he and his son would make the drop because Zell wanted to show his Jr. the ropes.

That night when Zell and his son rolled up to the spot to make the drop, the Feds rolled in thirty deep, I was told by the same detective that had been feeding me information. Instead of Zell cooperating, he decided to go out guns blazing. He told his son to take cover and not to come out. At first, he wanted to shoot it out with his dad, but Zell insisted. Zell counted to three, and his son dipped behind a brick wall. Zell, not being one to go to jail, decided to shoot it out with the police with his stupid ass.

I really hated this for my nigga, but like I said, it was either him or me. That same night, Zell's son was arrested and charged with possession of illegal substance, drug trafficking, trafficking cocaine, and possession of an illegal firearm. To make matters worse, I used my connect to make sure he got twenty years to life. The thing now was, why was he out early?

Beast was trying to come after my sons for something I did. Of course, he was smart, and knew I had something to do with what happened to his dad, that's why I became a snitch. Now I had to find a way to let my sons know that they were going through this bullshit because of the sins of their father. They could never find out that I basically snitched on my right hand's son.

Chapter 13

Eden

I thought I would have to bribe Jamison to let me up to Reeno's apartment, but he was actually eager to let me up. I didn't know what that was about, but hey. Jamison carried the groceries up that I had in my hand and then left me to myself.

I reached and turned the oven on so that it would preheat, I then went ahead and prepped my special meatloaf, garlic mashed potatoes, corn on the cob, and cornbread. I placed the pan with the meatloaf in the oven before heading to freshen up. I danced around to the music that was coming through the Beats speaker sitting on the bathroom counter.

My right foot was planted on the side of the tub as I shaved my pussy. Once finished, I washed myself again and got out the shower. I quickly applied shea butter to my skin, along with a little vanilla and almond oil from Bath and Body works before heading to the kitchen to check my food. I placed the cornbread in the oven because by the time it was done, the rest of my food would be ready to be taken out of the oven.

The food that I prepared was on the table. Reeno's apartment smelled garlicky like my mashed potatoes, but also sweet like my cornbread. I could hear the elevator rising as I hurriedly placed the salad I'd chopped up on the table.

I stood with my hands on my hip in my red bra and thongs as the elevator door opened. Reeno halted his steps upon seeing me. I didn't know how he would feel about seeing me in his place without his permission, so I stood there knowing I was looking sexy as hell. Shit, if he did feel some type of way, he wouldn't for long. I smiled as I watched him lick his fat ass lips while pulling on his beard. His gold bottom teeth shined as he broke out into a full smile.

"Damn, Ms. Eden. I can get used to this shit."

My red stilettos clicked across his hardwood floors. I stopped right in front of him and asked, "So you not mad I convinced Jamison to let me up?"

Reeno's arm circled my waist, his hands resting on my ass, and responded with, "Hell nah, Jamison knew you were cool. If it was anyone else, he would have turned them away. Plus, that nigga told me I had a surprise waiting, I knew it could only be you the way he was cheesing. I think he has a crush on your ass." He chuckled while I giggled.

I heard his stomach grumble, causing me to gaze up into his eyes. I pecked his lips then grabbed his hand. "Let's go take care of that, baby."

"I knew I smelled something good, and a nigga haven't eaten since breakfast."

"Why not? You have to eat; it's too hot outside for that."

He sat down while I filled his plate and grabbed two glasses to fill with sweet tea.

"I know, baby. I was just busy, and time got away from me."

He smacked my ass when I turned around to fix my own plate. I sat down, grabbing his hand so we could say grace. Once I did, we dug in, and I waited to see what he thought.

"Damn, woman. This shit on point."

He took a big bite of the garlic mashed potatoes, followed by the meatloaf. He then started on his salad. I guess he wanted to taste the actual meal first.

"This was a nice surprise, Eden. Thank you for this."

"I told you what I wanted tonight; I just came to get it."

Reeno sat back in his chair with his right hand on his stomach, I'm sure because he was full after eating two helpings.

"Well, let me take a quick shower, and I'll make good on that." He stood up, pulling me up with him and kissing my neck.

I went ahead and cleaned the kitchen, putting the extra food inside of the refrigerator for another time while he cleaned himself up. I was just prancing around while he was in the shower. I couldn't wait to feel him again. I looked down at his phone, which has rung for the third time in less than five minutes. My curiosity got the best of me as I picked his phone up, realizing that the number was not saved in his phone. The phone rang twice more before I looked toward the hallway to make sure he wasn't coming and answered his phone. I knew that was a big no-no, but I just had to know who, and why this person was blowing him up like this.

"Hello."

Silence. I took the phone away from my ear to see if the line was still connected.

"Hello." I sang into the phone.

"This better not be Reeno's phone you are answering."

"And is." I waited for the woman's next statement.

"Put him on the phone."

She demanded like she ruled something. The woman sounded as if she was gritting her teeth. I didn't care anything about that. I didn't know who she thought she was scaring. Shit, she on the damn phone for goodness sakes.

"Sorry, hun, he just finished the meal that I prepared for him in his house. Now he is taking a shower so he can eat this pussy and put me to sleep. May I take a message? Maybe I will let him call you tomorrow."

"Fuck you, hoe, just know that you won't be around for long once he hears what I have to say. Tell him to call A'Myracle."

Then she hung up. I erased the answered call along with the other times she called and placed his phone back on the counter where it was before I picked it up.

I knew that A'Myracle hoe wanted my man. Apparently, he didn't want her, because if he did, there would be no room for me. Oh well. I heard the shower water stop running, so I hurriedly wiped the sink down and made my way to the couch. I sat toward the end and draped my leg across the arm of the chair. I wanted this man right now. He was so fine I could just eat him alive.

I almost choked on my own spit when his ass walked back in here in all his glory, dick swanging from thigh to thigh, looking all delectable and shit.

"By the time I get to you, all that shit better be off."

He didn't have to tell me twice. I removed my bra, followed by my panties. I was about to kick off my shoes with my thong until he said, "Shoes on."

The way he said it had my fluids dripping down my ass crack and onto his couch. I was ready. He fell to the floor, yanking my legs to the end of the couch. All I remember is him licking between every crevice of my pussy and ass. The ceiling started spinning, that's how done he had me. Reeno slurped and sucked while pulling and tugging on my sweet pearl. I could be heard through the building as my voice traveled through the walls.

I released hard, and when I did, he spread my legs spread eagle style and entered me before my body came down from my high.

"Oooo, Reeno. Fuck me."

"Oh, you want all this dick?"

"Mm, yes."

I guess that turned him on, because the next thing I knew, he was fucking me long and hard. He pulled out and then scooped me up, carrying me to the large window that overlooked downtown Charlotte. He faced me toward the glass with my hands above my head, placed flat on the glass, and my little ass poking out. Reeno's finger entered my ass as his tongue whirled around it. I didn't know what this nigga was doing to me, but it was working.

I shivered as he turned me around, placing my back against the chilled window. My legs immediately circled his waist as he slowly entered my pussy. I was in heaven, feeling his long dick slide in and out of me slowly.

"Shit E, this pussy feels good, man. I'm not going to last much longer."

I couldn't even respond. All I knew was that I was on the brink of a release also.

"Grrrrrrr. Shiiiit."

He pulled out at the same time that he released, and I came also. My legs quivered while we stared at each other intensely. I was the first to smile, causing him to do the same.

He finally let me down, body still quaking, coming off my high. I was in heaven, and by the satisfied look on Reeno's face, he knew he did his thing.

We laid in his bed after taking a quick shower facing each other. My legs were tangled in his as my eyes kept closing. I was trying to stay up.

"Babe, if I wore you out that bad, just go to sleep. We can talk tomorrow." Reeno kissed my lips. The last thing I remember was his lips against mine, then I was asleep.

Destiny

My new friend Mace moved into his new home. He requested that I come over and have a celebratory drink with him. At first, I didn't think I should, but hey, I was a free woman. I didn't really want a drink because it was still before 5 p.m., so I let him know that I would come check things out.

From the looks of it, he had only furnished the living room and kitchen for now.

"I have to go now, Mace. I have somewhere I need to be," I told him as I sat my glass down.

"Do you have to go? I am enjoying your company."

Mace closed the gap between us on the couch. He licked my neck, causing my body to shiver. I had to go. I was not trying to sleep with this man. But damn, he was fine as fuck. My hand dropped on top of his lap from the weakness he caused throughout my body. I could feel his dick was thick as fuck. I jumped up with the quickness as his cocky ass laughed as his head fell back into the back of his couch. He jumped up quickly when he saw me headed to the door.

"Hold up, sweetheart."

"I have to go, Mace. Just call me later." I finally made it to the door.

"You really leaving a nigga?"

He backed me up to the door, causing me to look up at his tall frame. His lips were luscious, which were surrounded by his sexy ass mustache and beard. I licked my lips right before he bent down, pulling my lips into his mouth. I hated that he had me weak in the knees. His tongue played tug of war with mine until he finally pulled away.

"I'll see you another time then?" he questioned with his hand above my head.

I could barely think straight, but when I could, I let him know that he would. He stepped back, letting me out the door. I quickly walked out and hurried to my car. I breathed in deeply and released it slowly once I sat in the driver's seat. When I felt as if I could finally drive, I pulled off, headed to my office; I had a few clients to meet with.

I pulled up to my office building off of South Tryon Street, and parked near the entrance.

"Good afternoon, Destiny. Mr. and Mrs. Lakie are waiting for you over there in the lobby."

"Thank you, Christina." I continued to walk toward the lobby where I saw a couple who looked to be in their mid-thirties.

"Good evening. I am Destiny. Are you Mr. and Mrs. Lakie?"

"Yes, ma'am, a pleasure to meet you." They both held out their hands for me to shake. After shaking their hands, I led them both to my office to go over what they wanted for their first home.

******

My eyes rolled to the back of my head when I glanced down at my phone while driving home. Raydon had been calling all day, but I couldn't answer because I was busy. I rolled my eyes as I slid the green button across the screen to answer the phone.

"Yes, Raydon."

"I miss you, Destiny. I cannot stop thinking about your ass."

"Yeah right, Raydon. I don't want to hear it. You made your choice."

"Did I? Because I don't remember that. I remember telling you how much I wanted your ass."

"Raydon, I don't have time for this. You will be doing the same shit. Like I told you before, niggas are showing interest."

After I said that, I heard silence. I took my ear away from the phone and saw that he hung up. Shrugging my shoulders, I continued my way home. I didn't feel like hearing his shit anyway.

Twenty minutes later, I pulled up to my house, and of course, Raydon was sitting on my porch like he lived here.

Removing my keys from the ignition, I stepped out of the car and headed toward him. I continued past him, sticking my key inside the keyhole in order to unlock the door. I walked in and tried to close the door behind me, but of course, he grabbed it and made his way inside.

As soon as I dropped my things on the couch, I was being picked up and carried up the stairs.

"What the fuck, Raydon?"

"Nah, you want to talk all that bullshit about another nigga."

SMACK!

His hand came down on my bare ass because he had slid my skirt up. Damn, I hated when he did shit like this. It made it hard to resist him.

"I don't hear you talking that shit now." He dropped me down on the bed, standing before me as he removed every article of clothing that he had on.

I sat up and slid to the head of the bed, not wanting to get too close.

"I said what I said," I spoke softly as my eyes moved down to his thick rod, which he was currently massaging.

He chuckled before grabbing my foot and pulling me to the foot of the bed. He yanked my button-down shirt apart, causing all ten buttons to fling across the room. He then pulled my skirt down and ripped off my thongs.

"Raydon." My breathing sped up.

"You fucking him, Destiny?"

I didn't answer right away because I was admiring his body. But this shit wasn't going to change, either he commits or get the fuck from around here. He wasted no more time climbing on the bed and entering me swiftly as I screamed, trying to get adjusted to his width.

Chapter 14

Reeno

I stood in front of my brother, Zack, Chad, and two more of my most trusted hitters in a large room that only consisted of a long wooden table like what was used at the last supper. Other than us, the warehouse was empty. There was a monitor that took up a fourth of the wall with monitors hanging on the wall. It was there so that we could monitor the rest of the warehouse in and out, to make sure no one was sneaking up on us. Our cars were parked in an underground garage, so no one knew we were here.

The room was silent as everyone let the things I just said marinate in their brain. There was no room for mistakes tonight. We needed to be in and out. Because of Warren's information, we knew exactly where my people were being held.

I took a seat in front of my Mac-11 and loaded it with my extended clip. Seeing me do so caused everyone else to do the same with their weapon of choice.

"Remember, we don't know what we are walking into. I know my nigga said there were four of them, and I'm assuming those were the four that came to the car lot. But for real, we don't know who, or how many they may have guarding the place. If someone gets in the way, we splittin' they shit, no questions asked. Understood?"

Of course everyone nodded their heads in understanding. We were ready to go get our men, and nothing would stop us. I stood from my seat while saying, "Let's get it."

Me, Zack, and Chad hopped in one Tahoe, while Reeno and the other guys hopped in the second. All of our trucks we handled business in were bulletproof. We didn't have time for niggas trying to shoot us up while we were trying to get away.

We didn't have far to drive, just around the corner. We parked out of sight with our shoes hitting the pavement shortly after.

My adrenaline was rushing as we pulled our ski masks over our faces and split into our two groups; one taking the back, and the other taking the front. There were no entry points on either side of their building, so there was no need to cover it.

I spoke into our specialized Bluetooth walkie-talkies that sat inside our ears. My brother confirmed that he was ready.

"The door is unlocked, bro. No need to make noise kicking it in," Raydon confirmed.

I immediately checked my designated door and found this door was also open. These were some dumb ass niggas.

"Mine to Raydon. Let's get it. 5-4-3-2-1."

We both twisted the knob slowly, and once I counted to one, we were in there. Zack was the first to enter, followed by my third guy, and I came up the back. Across the floor, I saw my brother, Chad, and his third guy.

My eyes moved from left to right, noticing two guys blocking the door that we knew Warren, Vernon, and Latrell were in. We knew Latrell was dead, and I made a mental note to take care of the mother of his child and his mother. Just when I was pointing, one of them spotted us and stood, warning the others before letting off shots.

However, they didn't stand a chance against our automatic weapons. Raydon's team took them out while the two guys were focused on us. The way their heads exploded was comical. It looked as if a watermelon was burst wide open.

I made my way to the door while my team took out the other eight niggas that came from different points of the warehouse. I pulled the heavy door open and made my way downstairs. As soon as my guys came into view, I could see the relief on their faces.

"Let's go," I ordered.

Those few words lit fire under their asses. We made it to the top of the stairs and the gunfire had ceased. They stayed close until we got to the car, just in case more men came into view.

I heard a big ass explosion as we were pulling off. I looked at Zack and shook my head.

"Nigga."

"Hey, no face, no case." Zack shook his shoulders.

I chuckled as I drove to the club in silence. I didn't want to meet at the warehouse, that wouldn't be smart since apparently those sucka ass niggas knew where it was. I parked around back with Raydon pulling up close behind me. We entered the side door, making our way to the basement without anyone noticing we were there.

"Have a seat," I advised before taking my own seat.

Once seated, Warren was the first to speak.

"Thank you, man. I knew you would come through, I just wish Trell would have stuck with the plan." Warren shook his head,

"I'm going to make sure I handle his people. Now tell us who these niggas are and what their problem is." I focused on Warren and Vernon.

"Truthfully, they never said what the issue was; all I know is that they have it bad for you. Their names are Beast and Mace. Those are the main ones. The others we didn't get their names. But we saw them sprawled on the floor when we were leaving. Beast and Mace wasn't there."

I pulled out my phone and showed them a picture from my shop, and he confirmed that the picture was of Beast.

"OK." I stood up, walking toward the two. I placed a hand on each of their backs and said, "I'm glad you two are back. Go home and recoup. Holla at me in a few days."

Beast

I was livid, and somebody was going to pay for this shit. Me and Mace went to check on our little cousin because she was dealing with some shit, and I pulled up to my warehouse for it to be on fire. I couldn't tell if anyone was in there or not. All I knew was that firemen and at least three fire trucks were everywhere.

Not wanting to be associated to this shit, I pulled off and we went to my crib. As soon as we got there, I pulled up my security feed from the warehouse and watched as two trucks pulled up, and six niggas jumped out. A few minutes later, two extras came out with them.

"Fuck. It was fucking Reeno and them, bruh."

"How the fuck did they even know?" Mace asked. That was a great question because I had no idea how their asses knew anything. We were in that spot for a minute with no problems.

"What if it's only the two of us left? I'm sure all them niggas were in there."

Mace turned his head toward me, and I could see the worry in his eyes.

"What the fuck you mean? If that's the case, we handle these niggas ourselves. This nigga, Bear, ruined my fucking life. Then they kill bruh on some bullshit," I answered.

"But was it really bullshit, my nigga? We had him stealing from them folks. He got caught. We put bruh in that position. Him being dead is on us, whether you want to believe that or not," Mace spoke his mind.

"Who the fuck side you on, nigga?" I roared, getting upset at the fact that he was right, and I didn't want to accept it.

"Nigga, you know I'm right."

We placed Nelly in the crossfire. Before I even got out of prison, I had my little brother, Nelly to get in good with Reeno. See, I knew his father set up the night I got locked up, and my father killed himself.

Nelly and I had different mothers. Nelly was only eight when the shit went down. He reached out when he was old enough, and we came up with a plan to get back at Stanford. Since he was not in the game anymore, we planned on going after his sons. Shit, he let his best nigga's son go to jail, so why can't I set some shit up?

Stanford

A few nights later

My club was at full capacity. It was the weekend of the fourth of July, and everyone had come out to party. Every VIP space was taken, and my girls were tearing up the stage. Steven was doing a great job of holding things together.

"What's going on, Bear? I see you walking the floor today." A'Myracle greeted once she noticed me.

"Just for a few minutes, sweetheart. I know y'all got it."

"Yes, we do." She switched her ass off, making sure I saw that shit. My wife would whip her ass. Plus, I knew she is or was messing around with my son, Reeno. She better go on somewhere. I chuckled as I made my way to my office.

I waved to a few people that I passed by who spoke to me. Briggs hit me with a head nod as I passed the entrance of the place. Today was a great day until I walked into my office.

I stepped in and closed my door. I didn't know what this dude was thinking, but no one put fear in my heart, so if that's what he was trying to do, then he was as crazy as he looked coming into my place of business.

I walked around him until I was on my side of the desk. I unbuttoned my suit jacket before sitting down, and at that point, I acknowledged him.

"Beast, long time no see." I chuckled, not breaking eye contact with his young ass for a second. He wanted to play games with me,

I can show him what real games looked like; he should have left this shit alone.

"You would know exactly how much time that's been, wouldn't you?" Beast tilted his head to the side as he stood with his feet shoulder length apart and his arms folded.

I wasn't worried about his ass though. That's why I was still sitting. When he went to prison, he was just a jit. He didn't know enough to defeat me or my boys.

"What's your point of coming to my place of business?"

He took a second to gather his thoughts and sat in the seat in front of me.

"I just wanted to let you know to your face that I'm coming for y'all. You set my father up that night. It is because of you that he is dead, and I was sentenced to twenty years. I have infiltrated your organization in several ways. The most important was Nelly, but your sons murdered him. There is no body, but I'm sure of it. No one has heard from him in two months. You know anything about that?"

"What's done is done. I do not have to explain myself to you. It will be a very wise choice for you to get the fuck out of my club." I calmly stated.

Beast chortled as he stood from his seat and said, "You and your bastards watch ya backs. I see they finally found my warehouse. It took them long enough, considering I was right across the parking lot from them. They burned my shit to the ground. Let's see what I do next." With that said, Beast's weak ass walked out of the door. If he was going to kill me, I felt like he would have done it before he walked out that damn door.

******

The next night

I sat behind my large oak desk in my home office, waiting on my sons; my most prized possessions other than my wife. Taking a sip of my Crown Royal, I sighed, thinking about what I had to do. I just prayed that my boys understood that I did what I had to do. If I didn't, I would have left my wife to fend for herself with them.

"It will be OK, baby." My wife, Leena, stood behind me, massaging my shoulders. The shit felt good too.

Of course, she knew about what I did. She was the one who begged me to do it. All it took was her pleading with me while gazing into my eyes with her beautiful brown ones.

"I know, baby. I just hate that things are being fucked up because of something I did. This nigga should come after me, not my sons. But no, this bitch nigga trying to make me suffer."

I grabbed her hand, pulling her around the chair and into my lap. She placed both her hands on each side of my face and pecked my lips a few times. She smacked her lips, probably from the strong taste of that Crown. Laying her head on my shoulder, I caressed her back as she said, "Even if they are mad, you know they will still handle business."

That's one thing I did know about Reeno and Raydon. They damn sure were going to handle business, and if I needed to, I would be right beside them. We didn't speak another word because we heard the alarm chirp, indicating that someone had arrived, which of course, we knew it was our sons. My wife kissed me once more before rising off my lap just before Reeno and Raydon walked through my office door.

"Hey, ma." They both spoke, giving her a hug and then a kiss on the cheek.

"I will leave you all alone. If you need me, call for me." Leena looked directly at me, and I nodded my head. She left out, closing the door behind her

"What's up, Pops?" Reeno was the first one to speak and hug me. Afterward, they both sat down in front of my desk.

"So what's going on? What's so urgent that you called us over here?"

I stood up and went over to my mini bar. I fixed three shot glasses of Hennessy before giving one to each of my sons and keeping one to myself.

"Damn, this must be some shit," Reeno mumbled before downing his drink, right along with his brother, and then me.

"I've been keeping something from you. I didn't think it would ever come back around, but it has…"

Reeno and Raydon listened to me intently as I ran down everything that I knew. Even the parts about who Nelly was, and another possible infiltration.

I couldn't really tell what they thought by their facial expressions, because they made none. When I finished talking, the two stared at each other, and Raydon was the first to talk.

"Pops, man, all of this is because of some shit you did almost twenty years ago? This is some bullshit. We lost a good man from this bullshit. Nelly… Nelly. He was fake this whole time, man."

"What are you trying to do? We can't have this nigga poppin' up at clubs, car lots, nothing. Truthfully, I can't be mad at what you did because we wouldn't have been blessed to have you in our lives all this time," Reeno voiced what I already knew.

Reeno and Raydon took things better than I thought they would. I was glad them niggas didn't spaz out on me. I knew how they were, especially Reeno. Things could have gone a whole other way.

"I'm not sure what to do yet, but whatever it is, needs to happen soon," I spoke confidently.

Chapter 15

Raydon

I yawned as my eyes opened to be met with the strip of sunlight that snuck through the curtain in my room. I was tired as fuck after the night I had. After the revelation with my father, I made it a point to watch my back. Not only mine, but I followed Destiny a few times. I knew my brother had his people, and Stanford had my mother covered.

You never knew what these niggas were thinking. They would go after the person that you loved the most and not give a fuck about it. I had something for those niggas though. Who the fuck holds a twenty-year-old grudge? I mean, be thankful for your life nigga.

I swung my legs over my bed and stood to go and relieve myself. When I was done, I decided to go ahead and take a shower. I definitely needed one to wake me up.

I stepped out with a towel wrapped around my waist before treading into my room and grabbing the half-smoked blunt on my nightstand. Taking my first puff, it soothed my thoughts. However, they were interrupted by my phone ringing.

"What's up, bro?" I picked up for my brother who I hadn't spoken with since we were at my father's house.

"Aye, man, where you been the last few days?" My brother asked, sounding concerned. I knew he was, because we spoke every day, even if it was only for a second.

"I just been chillin', man. Nothing much. But it's crazy how you were right that Pops was hiding something."

"Yeah, but it's not as bad as I thought it would be. I'm glad he finally came clean though," Reeno stated.

We spoke on the phone for a little bit more before he asked to have lunch at the club. I didn't have a problem with that, because I was hungry as hell. Since we were meeting in an hour, it was no point to fix myself anything to eat.

A little over an hour later, myself and Reeno were sitting in a VIP area upstairs, waiting on our wings and Pepsi.

"Eden told me that her birthday is coming up. I wanted to have her something here. I know she doesn't have a lot of friends, but we can compensate for people."

"Yeah, get Destiny to invite some of her people from school, their old neighborhoods, all of that," I said.

"Yeah, you're right. We keeping this on the low, so don't go running your mouth, bruh-bruh." He chuckled, which I did the same.

"Nigga," I responded.

Steven bought our hot wings over with extra napkins and fresh sodas. Pops had some of the best wings at this club; I ate them whenever I chose to eat here.

Shortly after I left my brother, I found myself pulling up at Destiny's job. I saw her champagne-colored Mercedes E Class parked up front like it always was. I was about to get out of the car when I saw her walking out, and a dude got out of an all-black Cadillac SUV and walk toward her. I observed for a minute until I got a good look.

I pulled my phone out to get a picture of him. I made the camera appear to be taking a close up to him so that I could get a good look. This nigga looked familiar, and I hoped it wasn't who I thought it was. I waited a few minutes after sending the picture to Reeno so that he could confirm or deny what I thought.

I didn't get a text back; he called me which had me believing that this was serious.

"Yeah," I answered, once I slid the green phone across my screen.

"Fuck, that's one of the niggas who came to the car lot. Where the fuck are you?" Reeno questioned while I watched ol' boy speed out the parking lot and Destiny head back in her building with a bag in her hand.

"You won't believe this shit. I'm at Destiny's job. He got to her, bro. This is who she has been going out with. I fucked up, bro. I should have let her know my true feelings. It's not like I'm fucking off like I used to."

"Nah, don't even blame yourself. You know how this goes. They obviously been watching us and realized you cared about her. But don't worry. Let her know about it, and we will handle him," Reeno said.

Things always worked out in our favor, I just hated that Destiny was even put in this predicament. I was murdering whole families if anything happened to her. This time, I grabbed my phone, keys, and stepped out of my car. I headed to the entrance of her job, not giving a fuck about what she thought.

"Hi Mr. Brooks, Ms. Ryan is in her office. You can go on back,"

Destiny's secretary said. She was used to me coming there, considering I would bring food for the office most of the time.

"Thanks, sweetheart," I said, causing her ass to blush.

I walked down the hallway until I was in front of the one that belonged to Destiny. The door was wide open, so I walked straight in, but closed the door behind me. When she looked up, I could tell she wasn't happy. She smacked her teeth before asking, "What do you want, Raydon?"

I cut right to the chase, no need to beat around the fuckin' bush, "This nigga I just saw you with, what do you know about him?"

"I don't understand why that matters, Raydon, you had your chance."

"Destiny, I need to know if you know who he is. You know who I am, baby girl. I wouldn't be asking if it wasn't important."

She was really pissing me off today. Her ass needed to cooperate. Plus, I need to know that she's not helping this nigga.

"I need to know if you down with this nigga. Are you helping him set me and my family up?" I questioned, looking into her eyes, to her soul. She was confused and didn't know what I was talking about. I'm glad that shit got her attention.

"What are you talking about?" Her face was tight, and her mouth in a frown.

"That nigga using you to get to me, Destiny. You know how this shit goes."

She placed her pen down that she was holding, giving me her undivided attention. The next thing I knew, she laughed so loud I thought the windows would crack in her office. I frowned at her ass, not believing that she thought this was a game. I refused to believe that this nigga had her wrapped already. Her next words fucked me up.

"Raydon, get the fuck out," she seethed.

"Des, baby, look at me…" I took a few seconds to let her glare into my eyes before continuing, "I'm not bullshittin'. Everything that had been happening to me and Reeno, had been because of him and some nigga named Beast in retaliation to some shit my father did damn near twenty years ago. You need to listen to me, baby. Even though we are not on good terms, I'm not going to let anything happen to your ass. Now, what's his name?"

I saw the wheels turning in her head. She was thinking about what I was sayin', but she still wasn't sure. That shit fucked me up. I thought me and her were better than that.

"Raydon…"

"Keep rollin' those eyes, and I will knock them shits out your fuckin' sockets." I gritted my teeth at her ass as I stood up.

I turned toward the door and marched toward it, stopping right when I had my hand on the knob. I turned, facing her so that she could hear me clearly.

"I am very disappointed in you, Des. You should know that I would never steer you in the wrong direction. This shit goes to show that you don't know my ass at all. When you see that nigga's true colors… It doesn't even matter." I didn't even finish my sentence; she wasn't even taking me seriously. I slammed the door on my way out and walked out of the building.

Destiny

Raydon's ass thought he was slick. He was making up that bullshit, just so I can stop talking to my new friend. Right? I swirled around in my swivel chair to face my window. My head fell to the back of the chair as I closed my eyes, questioning my thoughts for a minute.

I wouldn't think that he would steer me in the wrong, but the fact that I warned him that I would start talking to other people should have told Raydon I wasn't playing with his ass. He must've wanted me to be miserable while he went ahead, fucking these bitches.

I turned back around, noticing it was time for me to leave and show a house. I let out an exaggerated breath as I stood to my feet and grabbed my briefcase, purse, phone, and keys. I headed out, letting my secretary know that she would have to lock up because I wouldn't be coming back.

The shit Raydon was saying was on my mind. I needed to see if the things he was saying about Mace were true. I picked up my phone and dialed his number before pulling off.

"What's up, ma?" Mace answered the phone with his heavy New York accent.

"Hey, Mace. I'm on the way to show a house but I have a quick question."

"Ask me anything."

"Do you know somebody named Beast?"

It was a quick pause before he said, "Nah, what made you ask me that?"

I didn't know if I should let him know what was going on or not. I mean, he seemed to be harmless. I hadn't had any issue with him in this short amount of time that I've known him.

"It's nothing. My ex was just asking about you. He asked if you knew that person. He probably just thought he recognized your face. He was pulling up while you were leaving my building."

"Tell that nigga don't worry about me, he must be mad that I caught yo' fine ass." I could hear the smile in his voice. Raydon was crazy. Ain't nothing wrong with this nigga.

"Hey, how about I pack a bag and come to your house tonight?" I questioned.

"I will damn sure love that shit," he responded, sounding just as happy as me.

"I'll see you then, babe."

Later that night

The sun had just set when I pulled up to Mace's house. "Get it together, girl," I spoke out loud. I was nervous not knowing how tonight would go. This would be my first time spending the night.

I was about to step out of the car when my phone rang. It was Eden, so I answered quickly before I got out my car.

"Hey, babe."

"Girl, what you up to?"

"I'm at Mace's house, girl. He finally talked me into staying the night."

"Oh my god, so you and Raydon are really over? We haven't really seen each other since I've been pretty much staying at Reeno's house," Eden asked.

"Yeah, I know. We've both been doing our own thing. But Raydon made his choice. His ass doesn't want to commit, sooo…" I shrugged my shoulders as if Eden could see me.

"Damn, I'm sorry, cuz. I know you really love him. But I'm going to let you go spend time with the new boo. But look, I don't know that nigga. Send me his address."

"OK boo, sending it as soon as I hang up." I did just that. I knew she was just worried since I didn't know dude that well.

I finally stepped out of my car and made my way up his circular driveway. Before I even made it to the porch, the door swung open, but it wasn't Mace who answered. It was a muscular dark-skinned guy, who tried to have a pleasant look on his face, but it wasn't working. He had a New York hat on his head with a white t-shirt.

"Hey," I spoke nervously.

"You must be, Destiny. Mace told me all about you. He is upstairs; he'll be down in a minute. Come on in."

He held the door open wide enough for me to step inside. I sighed under my breath feeling better that Mace was upstairs. I turned toward him and asked, "Hey, what's your name? You know mine, but I don't know yours."

The guy smirked just as I saw Mace headed this way from the staircase. All thirty-two teeth were showing until the guy said, "Beast."

"Shit," I whispered as I dropped my bags and tried to make a run for the front door.

Chapter 16
Reeno

Two days later

Now that I knew where the base of our problem was, I knew what and who to look for, for the most part. I made sure someone was always in the background ready for whatever. We hadn't heard anything since that nigga's warehouse was blown to smithereens.

I glanced down at my diamond filled Rolex, noticing it was almost five o'clock. It was Monday, and we spent a few hours before opening counting fucking inventory. I hated doing this shit, but my pops made it mandatory that everyone be here; well, everyone except the strippers. They don't have shit to count.

Knock, Knock!

I glanced up from my computer to see A'Myracle dressed in a pair of jean shorts that looked like they were stopping her pussy from breathing. She had on a crop top to match, and she looked damn good. I'd been avoiding her since the day she was naked in my office. I wasn't sure what she wanted.

"Yeah." I placed my pen down and flipped the papers over that I was reading.

"Hey, can we talk?" She waited by the door until I said that it was OK for her to enter. She walked in, closing the door behind her. She then sat her ass in the chair in front of my desk.

"What you want to talk about, A'Myracle?"

"Us."

I couldn't do anything but shake my head at her ass. She just didn't get it. I sat back in my chair and said,
"I thought we went over this? You cool as fuck, but there is no us, baby girl. Don't make this shit hard on yourself."

"But things were good before you met that skinny bitch."

"A," My deep voice traveled through my office. I cocked my head to the side and made sure she heard me loud and clear. "Don't call my girl a bitch. That woman hasn't done anything to you for you to be disrespecting her like that."

Of course, she got an attitude, rolling her eyes and neck like that shit hurt me. I didn't give a fuck about that shit.

"Well, it's true." She crossed her arms.

"You should have known this little thing wasn't going to last forever. We only fucked when I wanted to. We never went anywhere, so I'm confused at how you have any feelings for me. I'm done with the conversation; I'm not dealing with this shit. I have work to do, and so does your ass."

"But I…"

"Nah…" I held my hand up to stop her as I shook my head and responded, "No buts, A'Myracle. We can still be cool around here. I don't want this shit to be awkward, a'ight?" I questioned, not wanting any confusion between the two of us. I mean, shit, she was cool as fuck, but she was not the one.

"I guess." She stood and stormed out of my office. I didn't know if she heard me or not, but hopefully, she knew not to fuck with me. If not, she'd learn.

I spent the next thirty minutes counting our liquor and then keying the shit into the system on my computer. I swear, I could never get a minute to myself, because every fuckin' time I sat down, somebody was knocking the door down.

"Come in, damn," I answered, aggravated until I saw who it was, then I straightened up quick.

"Oh shit, Pops. My bad. What's up?" I gave him my undivided attention.

"Damn, son, who were you expectin'?"

"Man, A'Myracle's ass."

"I told you not to mess around with her, son. First, y'all damn near work together. It is going to be awkward between you two now. She is not going to know how to handle you cutting her off."

"Yeah, I know, man. But I'm not trying to go there with her anymore, I can't," I expressed to my pops as my head rolled forward while my hand went to my chin before lifting my head back up. "I'm really feelin' Eden, and I'm not trying to fuck shit up."

My father took a pull of his cigar before pushing the smoke through his lips and letting it flow through the air. I poured myself a shot of Hennessy from the bottle that was on my desk and downed it just as I heard my father's deep laughter.

"You got it bad, son," he spoke, just as my text alert went off.

I guess a nigga must have been cheesin' like hell because he started crackin' jokes on my ass. That nigga swore I was in love now.

"Nah, it's not love yet, but it's getting there. Eden is heaven sent. She is smart as shit, has her own career and everything. She lives with her cousin right now, but that's just because she just moved back to Charlotte from Durham. She went to Carolina."

"Oh, OK, she's a Tar Heel. I like her already. Why don't you and Raydon bring y'all women by the house one weekend for dinner?"

"Well, I can, pops. But Raydon's girl gave him an ultimatum, and you can guess which way that went. He's not ready to commit."

"Welp, that's your brother. But look, I came in here to say again that I'm sorry for putting y'all in this predicament. I can tell y'all that he ain't got shit on y'all. This nigga been locked up over half of his life, he doesn't even know how this shit works. He stuck in the old times. Just watch your back, I feel that's the only way that he can get the one up on any of us."

"You good, pop. I mean, I may not agree with how you did things, but you my father. Fuck the rest. I still love you."

I stood to my feet, walked around my desk to grab him up, and give him a hug. Once I sat back at my desk, my phone rang. It was Eden, so I went ahead and answered.

"What's up, baby girl?"

"Reeno, I'm really worried about Destiny. She met a dude a few weeks ago. She went to visit him two days ago and haven't been home. Can you ask Raydon if he has talked to her? I know they on bad terms, but maybe he can help."

My pop got up, going to get Raydon from his office and returned with him. I explained what Eden said to me, and I could see the anger on his face. Not only anger but worry.

Bruh was upset as he spoke, "I told her he was the enemy, and she didn't believe me. Tell Eden we are on the way to her house."

Eden

These past few days I have been focusing on planning for the school year. I only had a few more weeks before school started. I yawned as I stretched my legs out on the bed.

I picked up my phone to see if Destiny texted me back yet. When she didn't, I began to worry. Destiny and I are close and have never went a day, or at least every other day, without talking to each other. This new nigga she met was questionable. Who keeps a woman for days and not let her call her family? I knew it was his ass because cuzo wouldn't do that to me. She knew I was always worried.

I picked up my cell phone, not being able to hold it in anymore. I let Reeno know what I was thinking so that he could tell Raydon. They were meeting me at the house in a few.

I headed downstairs to get a bottle of orange Twist. On my way out of the kitchen, the doorbell rang. I knew it was Reeno and them, but I still glared through the peephole. As soon as I opened the door, Reeno's sexy ass grabbed a hold of me, engulfing my body with his arms.

"Hey, baby," he greeted.

"We ain't got time for the bullshit. What the fuck did this dumb ass girl do?" Raydon's ass asked as he strode into the living room and sat down on the couch.

"Why are you talking about my girl like that?" I asked him.

"Because, I saw her with that nigga Mace the other day, and I told her ass that he was the enemy, and she needed to stop fuckin' with his ass. Shorty said fuck me and made me leave her job. I have never steered her ass wrong."

"Damn, bro."

"Oh my god." My feet tread across the carpet as I bolted upstairs. I searched for my phone, which I found it on my bed where I left it. I hurried back downstairs to show them the address.

"She texted me his address. I almost forgot about it." I handed my phone to Raydon who studied the address.

"Fuuuck. I can't believe this shit. Bro, let's go check this shit out. Thank you, Eden."

"No problem. Bring my girl home."

"Hopefully her ass will listen to me next time. She should know a nigga would never steer her wrong."

I could see that Raydon was hurt that Destiny didn't have faith in him. I also saw a hint of doubt. He didn't think he would get to her in time. I swear, I prayed she was OK. Reeno and Raydon left out of the house in hopes of the next time we saw each other, it would be with my cousin in tow.

Chapter 17

Destiny

"Please stop, I don't know shit about that part of his life." My lips trembled, and my body shuddered as tears flowed down my cheeks, landing under my chin as this big ugly nigga quizzed me with the same questions that he'd been asking for the past two days. Although I was petrified, I kept eye contact with him, hoping that he could see that I was telling the truth. I really didn't know anything about Raydon's illegal dealings. He would never include me in them, and I was never interested in them either.

My eyes left Beast as I frowned at Mace, who glared at me like he didn't give a damn that he played me. I couldn't believe I fell for his shit. I guess my judgment was clouded because I was pissed at Raydon. But right about now, I would feel exultant to see his ass. The only glimmer of hope that I had of getting out of this was the fact that Eden had this address. I was praying that she gave it to Reeno to come find me.

"Bitch, I don't know why you going through this for him. That nigga don't even care about you enough to make you his girl."

My head snapped back to Mace. He apparently told this nigga all my damn business. I swear, if I got out of this, I wanted to handle him my damn self. Mace was a pussy. He hadn't said anything this whole time. All he did was do everything that this Beast character told him to do. He went to get their food, drinks, check on their businesses, every freaking thing. My head turned back toward Beast as he yelled in my ear, causing me to jump. His hand slapped me hard on my thigh.

He had me tied to the bed in my bra and panties. I didn't see the point of the shit. I think they did it to scare me, and it worked at first.

"When he finds me, he is going to kill both your asses." I made Beast angry and got hit in the face again. I could feel it swelling, but my face didn't hurt that bad.

"You know, you have a smart-ass mouth, maybe we should teach her a lesson, Mace." Beast stood to his feet as he glanced over at Mace, who had a smile on his face like he had been ready.

I instinctively closed my legs tight, crossing my ankles as my head shook side to side. My ass spoke too soon, these niggas were crazy. I closed my eyes tightly, praying for God to save me. I didn't deserve this at all.

"Why would you want to do something so foul? I haven't done anything to either one of y'all."

"It happens like that sometimes when you play in our game. He should have kept you safe, but he didn't because he's lame as fuck. If my man was able to take your attention away from him, then he wasn't worth your time, baby girl," Beast said as he sat on the bed beside me while his hands made their way up and down my thighs.

"Leave, my nigga," he directed Mace without looking at him.

"What?" Mace grilled Beast like he was offended. This time, Beast turned his head and repeated himself. This time, Mace got up and left the room, saying how fucked up it was that he didn't get me first since he was the one who got me there. That was some fucked up shit to think. Like, who gets mad because they don't get to rape someone first? I never heard of any shit like that.

"Don't do this, please. I swear to God, I don't know anything." I twisted and turned my body, even though I couldn't go anywhere because my hands were tied to the headboard.

He didn't say anything; his hand traveled down and made its way inside of my panties. I saw this look in his eyes as he toyed with my clit, attempting to rouse me. But really, he must not have known how this sex thing worked, because I was in no way turned on. I was actually scared shitless.

Sweat formed on my forehead as I whimpered, not wanting to partake in whatever he was about to do.

"Stop, please! Ahhhhhh!" I tried making as much noise as I could, but that only made him mad, causing me to get hit in my face again. My ears rang from his hand slipping and hitting my ear. I didn't want to get hit anymore, so I continued to whimper as he assaulted my body while I prayed for a distraction. It seemed as if that prayer was never answered. I felt the dip in the bed disappear, followed by a belt buckle hitting the hardwood floor.

"No, no, no, please."

I couldn't believe this was happening to me. I couldn't even fight the way I wanted since my hands were tied. The bed dipped back down as Beast hooked his fingers onto my panties and yanked them off. I was screaming, yelling, and kicking my legs, but in the end, he took control. He was strong and held my legs to my ears as he licked my pussy, causing me to throw up in my mouth. The chunky substance oozed down the sides of my cheeks as I cried. Beast lifted up, and the next thing I knew, he was hovering over me with his dick at my entrance. Fuck my life.

Raydon

You would think my head was on fire the way smoke was rising from my nose. My fists clenched, and my leg shook as Reeno drove like a bat out of hell to the hood so that we could grab a low-key car and some other things we may need.

"Fuck, fuck, fuck!" I shouted as I repeatedly punched the dashboard, upset with myself for not kidnapping her ass and keeping her at my place.

"Calm down, bro," I heard Reeno comment through my rant.

"How can I calm down, bro? I fucked up, I fucked up bad. I warned her, which meant that I knew this could happen. I should have made her listen to me. But I will take that. I just hope my girl OK."

"Oh, now she your girl?"

"Hell fuckin' yeah, she is. I don't care if we not fuckin' with each other like that right now. This nigga gonna get his for real." I nodded my head up and down as I spoke. I wasn't playin' no games. Mothafuckas wanted to play with the Brooks brothers, then I was gonna show them what I was really about. I turned toward my brother so he could understand what I was saying.

"I feel you, bro, but don't blame yourself; it's that punk ass nigga that is to blame. He lame as fuck for pullin' this shit. But on some real shit, we going to get your girl back. That's sis, and nobody fucks with her," Reeno said as he pulled up to a house off Sugar Creek Rd near WT Harris Blvd.

He opened the garage and pulled in. We both got out of the car and entered the house once the garage was closed. This was a little house that we kept to store little shit we needed. Just know, if the police ever found this house, we'd be in prison or dead. A couple lived here that we paid so the house wouldn't look deserted. Someone on the outside looking in would think they were a regular family, but for real, they were broke as shit. We grabbed the tools we needed, changed into all black, and then was back in the garage, stepping inside an all-black Cutlass Supreme.

Reeno drove past the address that Eden gave us. There were only two lights on in the house, and there were two cars in the driveway. I knew for a fact, one of them was at my car lot that day. Once we pulled down the dark street, we backed up into the driveway of a vacant house. No one was outside, so we weren't worried about anyone seeing us. If someone did want to stick their nose in our shit, then they would suffer the consequences.

"What's the plan, bro? I'm following you on this," Reeno asked.

"Shit, I want to just burst through that shit, but I know we need to feel the place out first," I responded.

"Yeah, we do need to keep a level-head with this shit. The wrong move could hurt a lot of people." He looked at me seriously. It was crazy because he was normally the one wanting to fly off the handle, and I was usually the one who kept his head on straight.

I reached into the back seat and grabbed my bag. I opened it and pulled out the shit I needed. I had to see if I could get a peek inside the house. Holding the binoculars up to my eyes, I searched through every single window. I couldn't spot Destiny anywhere, but I did spot those fuck ass niggas.

"There those niggas go, window in the right corner." I rattled off to Reeno, who lifted his own pair of binoculars, turning toward where I told him to look.

We sat and watched that nigga Mace for hours come and go, which meant, Beast was inside with baby girl. My eyes moved to the time on the radio, seeing that it was three in the morning. I had just witnessed Beast leave in his Cadillac. I sat up and hit my brother in the chest, letting him know that it was time to go.

"Nigga, Beast just left. I say we go up in there now. It's killing me."

"Say no more bro."

■ ■

These had to be some of the dumbest criminals I know. Me and Reeno walked right through the back door. We took turns going from room to room with our guns leading the way, making sure there was no one downstairs. Next, I led the way upstairs and began searching those rooms. I abruptly stopped, holding my left hand up, indicating for Reeno to stop. When I heard Destiny whimpering, I looked back at Reeno, who already knew what it was.

I made my way to the cracked door where I was hearing her voice. I stopped in my tracks, my lip curled, and my finger inched closer to the trigger. I motioned for my brother to come look, and I witnessed his whole face turn red. I hurriedly pushed the door open before he made his next move. Destiny looked at me, and I shook my head for her not to alarm Mace.

He was between her legs, licking her pussy butt ass naked, and you could tell she didn't want him doing that shit.

"I bet you better get your bitch ass up," I stated calmly.

Mace jumped so high that I thought the top of his head was going to touch the ceiling. He stood wide-eyed, waiting to see what was going to happen next. It looked as if he wanted to capitulate, but we were way past that shit.

"Go get your girl. I got this." Reeno pointed his gun at Mace.

I holstered my gun, moving toward the bed. I pulled out a pocket knife, cutting the zip ties off of her wrists as I told her, "I'm here, baby. I got you."

Destiny's hair was all over her head, and I could see the purple marks on her cheeks and eye. Dried blood was caked below her lip, and the dried-up semen on her right thigh was an indication of what she endured.

I couldn't stop my eyes from misting over. I wanted her to know that a nigga was for real, so I made sure to keep eye contact with her. Her body shivered as I carried her in my arm to the door. Her head fell on my shoulder as she cried.

"Bro, you want to take care of this?"

"No. No please, it was all Beast," Mace pleaded.

I nodded to my brother, instructing him to handle it. I didn't have time to listen to the bullshit he was spittin'. I continued toward the stairs, hearing a gunshot before feeling my brother's presence behind me. We left the same way we came. Once we got to the car, Raydon opened the back door for me to get in with Destiny, before heading to the driver's side and getting in.

"Raydon, I'm sorry I didn't believe you."

"Shhhhh. It's OK. Don't cry, baby. I'm here now." I used my hand to move her hair from her face. I just wanted to get her home, clean her up, and see if she felt like talking about what happened.

Chapter 18

Beast

I had to step out after feeling some of that pussy. Destiny's pussy was A1; I see why Raydon kept her around. That shit tasted even better.

People would probably say that I was crazy for holding this grudge over twenty years, but nah, when you in prison for that long, you don't have anything else to think about. I thought about Stanford all these years. Even when his sons were of age, I kept up with them too.

They've killed all my men except for Mace, and my other Ace in the hole. I just have to get her ass straight. She acted like she didn't know how to make that pussy work. That was the key to gettin' these niggas; pussy.

I knew they would come for Destiny, and when they did, me and my nigga would be waiting for they asses. The blaring ringing of my phone filled the car, causing me to reach for it.

The fuck does she want? I thought, looking down at the name.

"Yeah?"

"What's up, cuzo?" My cousin responded.

"Nothing much, I hope you back on that, baby girl?"

"Naw, he has been ignoring me. I really don't know what to do at this point."

"I don't give a fuck what you do at this point. Shit, you know where he lives, show up at his condo," I told her ass. I'm getting sick of all the excuses.

"OK, I will try that. Bye."

She hung up on me, probably because I sounded agitated.

Finally pulling up on the street where Mace lived, I saw an old school black car speeding by. I didn't know what that was about, but they didn't need to be speeding in this residential area.

As I walked through the front door, chills ran down my spine. I could feel that something was off.

"Aye, yo, Mace, where ya at?"

Silence.

"My nigga?"

I don't know why this nigga wasn't answering me. Then it popped into my head as it shook, thinking about Destiny. This fool was definitely getting some pussy. I made my way up the stairs, two at a time, wanting to burst through the room on their asses. However, when I opened the door, I couldn't stand the sight before me. My stomach churned, and I could feel throw-up at the back of my throat. My nigga was laid out naked with several bullet holes from his head down to his waist. His fuckin' dick was even shot off. Who takes the time to shoot off somebody's dick? It was apparent that he was fucking that bitch, and the nigga got in his feelings.

"Shiiit."

What the fuck was happening around me? When I was in prison, I just knew I'd thought everything out. I had counted everything that could go wrong, and just knew I could out-think these niggas. I looked down at my homie since we were kids and got pissed at myself. I felt like I set him up for failure.

"Let me get the fuck out of here," I said out loud.

Yes, I was fucked up that I had to see this nigga like that, and yes, my feelings were hurt, but he was dead, and there's nothing I can do about it.

*****

Sitting on my couch, I switched between taking gulps of Absolut and pulling on a blunt of Kush. I repeated this for a few hours before I decided to head up to my bedroom. I was always careful about coming to where I actually laid my head. Even if someone did follow me, they would have a hard time getting through my gates.

Removing my shoes, followed by my sweats and t-shirt, my head was spinning from all the drugs I'd consumed, plus the things that had been going on in my life. Nothing had gone as planned. I just hoped that things fell into place soon.

Chapter 19

Reeno

Eden looked fine as fuck sitting at the table by the window in my living room. I stood with my back against my kitchen counter with my legs crossed at the ankles as I sipped on a glass of cran-apple juice. I couldn't keep my eyes off of her doing something simple as getting her lesson plans together. A pen was between her luscious lips, being held in place by her teeth. Her hair was piled on the top of her head as she sat with her back straight and legs crossed. Her silhouette against Charlotte's skyline was dope as fuck.

After what happened to her cousin, she didn't talk much. She only wanted to make sure Destiny was OK, and I respected her for that. Eden finally agreed to come home with me when Raydon promised to take care of Destiny.

She glanced over at me, smiling, causing my head to tilt to the side as I made my way over to her. I placed my hands on her shoulder and squeezed gently, causing her to rotate her shoulders. She'd been at this all morning, and I was sure she needed a break.

"How about you chill out for a minute? I know you're hungry or something. I made you lunch. Come on." I held my hand out as I waited for her to place her pen down. Once she did, she grabbed my hand and I pulled her close to me.

"You are amazing," she said to me.

"Oh yeah, what I do?"

She pecked my lips before saying, "I just love the fact that you risked yourself for my cousin. I know Raydon is your brother, but you didn't have to do that. I also love how attentive you are to me." She looked up into my eyes as her weight shifted from one foot to another. It was cute.

"You fuckin' with a real G, Eden." I pecked her once more, making her smile before leading her to the kitchen. She giggled, smacking me on my shoulder as she said, "Boy, hush." But she just didn't know that she really was fuckin' with a real nigga.

"What do you have planned today?" she asked me before taking a bite of her turkey sandwich.

"I have something planned for us."

"For us?"

I chuckled as her eyes stretched wide.

"Yes, for us. Look E, I didn't want to say anything at first, because we didn't know each other like that, but you need a new car babe. That putt-putt ass Honda not working."

Her mouth was wide open in shock while I couldn't stop laughing. "What?"

"You know you don't have to do all that for me, Reeno."

"Oh, I know I don't, but I want to."

This time she broke out in a smile.

- -

Eden and I sat in my homeboy's office, who was the manager at Hendrick BMW dealership we were at. When I asked Eden what type of car she wanted, this is what she told me.

"All you have to do is sign your name here, here, and here." Alphonzo pointed.

Eden sat there for a minute and then looked up at me, "You're not going to sign?"

"No, sweetheart. This is your car, you sign."

He eyes bucked as she picked up the pen and started signing her name. When she was finished, she turned toward me with that beautiful smile.

"Thank you so much, baby."

"You deserve it."

"Here are your copies and your keys." Alphonzo handed the keys to Eden who hurriedly jumped up to go check out her brand-new white BMW X3.

I stood back and watched my baby jump up and down in bliss once she reached the car that was parked right up front. I caught up to her, opening the door for her to admire the inside. Her hand glided across the wood grain interior. Her ass sat in the leather seat on the driver's side, ready to roll. After I kissed her, she thanked me for what felt like a million times before I got into my car and followed her out of the parking lot.

Chapter 20

Raydon

Three days… It's been three days since I got my baby up out of that shit. It took a minute, but she told me what that bitch nigga did to her. I couldn't wait to catch and kill Beast's hoe ass.

I stood up and headed toward the kitchen, sitting my glass on the counter before making my way into the bedroom where Destiny was.

"You straight, babe? You hungry or anything?" I asked her, knowing she was tired of me asking if she was OK or if she needed anything, but I felt obligated.

"I'm fine, Raydon. I promise," she responded solemnly.

She was focused on the TV. I knew her ass was lying because I was now lying next to her, staring at her ass and she wouldn't look my way. It had been like that since we got here. I calmed her down the best I could while giving her a bath, then helping her get dressed. Eden was here helping for a while, but thankfully, I got her to leave. I wanted to be the one that catered to her.

Once I got her talking, she expressed that she wanted to go to her doctor to get an STD test. She called the very next day, and since she was a regular patient, the receptionist made her an appointment the same day. Now we were waiting for the results.

"Do you look at me differently now?" I heard Destiny ask in a monotone. She covered her face with her hands, waiting for my answer.

It hurt a nigga's heart for her to think like that. I risked my life, along with getting my brother to risk his for her. You don't do that for people you don't care about. I lifted my head, resting it on my hand to elevate my head a little as I gently pulled her hands away from her face. I then lifted her chin so that she could hear what the hell I was about to say. I hated how these niggas broke her in ways that she had to be put back together. That's OK though. I was here for it all.

"No, baby. I don't look at you differently. What happened to you is not your fault. In fact, a nigga blames himself. I should have made you listen to my ass. Just know that I'm here." I placed my forehead against hers as she began to cry again.

This shit was tugging at my heartstrings. A thug almost shed a tear. Those shits were sitting on the rim of my eyes, but I didn't want them to fall.

"Shhhhh. I got you." I kissed her gently all over her bruised face. This shit made me not want to let her out of my sight again.

"How is she?"

Eden hugged me as she waited for my answer.

"The same as she has been. Thanks for bringing these things over, she not leaving this house no matter what."

"She upstairs?" Eden questioned.

I nodded my head, causing her to head upstairs. Hopefully, Eden could cheer her up a little bit. When I tried to cheer her up, she told me she wouldn't feel right until I handled Beast. When she said that, it had a nigga fucked up. She had never talked like that before. But people don't realize when you do hateful shit to people, karma was a bigger bitch than you... and I was going to be that bitch as soon as he was found.

Reeno

"Mario, these cars just came in. There is a list of everything that needs to be done on the front seat of each car."

"Yes, boss man." My mechanic walked off with an understanding of what he needed to do.

I stood at the front window to make sure the five cars we purchased at the auction earlier this morning were being parked where they needed to be parked. When I was sure that they listened to what I said, I made my way to my office. I sat behind my desk and heard a knock. I was about to curse Angel out but realized it was Eden.

Her ass knew she was sexy walking up in here with that short ass dress on. I grabbed my dick because it was rising.

"Damn." I jumped out my seat and made my way over to her smiling ass.

"I'm glad you wearing that dress," I told her as I turned her around and pulled her panties down.

My finger went to the folds of her pussy, and she was already ready for a nigga.

"Damn, E." She must have wanted it as much as me because, at that point, she was ripping my damn clothes off.

We both stood naked before I lifted her on top of my desk, holding her legs apart as my head dipped down to lap her juices up. They were already oozing. I continued to attack her clit by whirling my tongue around. Her hand moved to my head as she tugged at my hair, trying to bury my face in deeper into her pussy. A nigga not bragging, but I was confident in my skills.

"Ooooo, Reeno."

I loved the way she bit her lip after screaming my name as her body shuddered. Once her body calmed down, I kissed her stomach, followed by her breasts, and ended at her lips.

I pulled her to the edge of the desk and entered her slowly. Once inside her warmness, I sped up my pace as she held on to my neck. I'm sure Angel could hear our moans and skin slapping. Shiiit, I didn't care though. Pulling out, I stood her to her feet and turned her around, bending her over the desk. I dove right back in and pounded her until we both exploded.

"Shit, girl. You came here 'cause you knew I needed this." I pecked her once on the lips before sitting up.

We both went over to the sink in my office and cleaned off the best we could. I sat in my chair, pulling her on my lap.

"What you doing over here for real though?"

"I can't see you?" She pouted.

I slapped her thigh while saying, "Of course your fine ass can."

"I just wanted to see you before I went to your house to get more work done. Plus, I wanted to see what you had planned for my birthday."

"If I tell your ass, it won't be a surprise. Be patient, baby."

Her lip poked out again, but she knew she had to wait. I had to make sure everything was perfect for E. I had to take care of a couple of things. I kissed her neck but noticed she was staring into space like something was bothering her.

"What's up? You good?"

She turned her head, facing me, and took a few seconds before she answered by saying, "What's up with you and A'Myracle?"

I felt my face ball up at the question, wondering why she was even asking me that shit. I guess it took too long for me to answer because she stood her little ass up and was heading toward the door. She had her hand on the knob when I finally snapped out of it and caught up to her.

"E, what you doing?" I held on to her wrist.

"You fuckin' her? I can't believe your ass. Let me go."

She tried to get out of my grip, but I pulled her into a bear hug and confessed, "I haven't fucked her in a minute. Not since we've been talking. That's why her ass be giving me the evil eye and shit. I haven't even been talking to her. I swear to God."

She stopped struggling against me, but when she turned around, I saw tears. I pulled her closer and kissed away every single one.

"You promise?" was the only thing she asked.

"I do, baby. I wouldn't lie to you. Did she say something to you or something?"

"Please don't be mad at me."

She was staring at me with puppy dog ass eyes like she really did some shit. I wasn't sure where she was going with this, but I said I wouldn't be mad at her, so I wouldn't.

"She called your phone a while back while you were in the shower. I picked up, and she was telling me how I was only temporary, and you would always be hers. She told me you would be back in her pussy when you were tired of mine."

I shook my head, not even wanting to respond to the shit A'Myracle said. That girl was really trippin'.

"Nah, baby. I'm not mad you answered my phone. What's mine is yours, baby. And as far as her, she wishes she could have me, but nah, you the one, baby. She was just a placeholder until I met my dope ass future."

I placed my hand on her chin, pulling her in and placing my lips against hers. I backed her up to the wall because I needed to give her more of this monster. It didn't take long for me to loosen my belt and push my pants down a little to free myself. Next thing I knew, I was pushing inside of *my* pussy, giving Eden those long death strokes right there on the wall.

Chapter 21

Destiny

One Week Later

Something happens inside your mind when you have someone steal something so precious to you. At the time, I felt myself close off. I had no emotions when he was on top of me. A woman's vagina is one of the most sacred places on her body. That lame nigga tried to leave a black hole in my soul. I had sat around enough. I had to get up and get out or he would win. Eden was right when she was over here. I needed to hang out. Maybe I would go get my nails and toes done with her as she suggested. Shoot, that was a start.

The good thing about all of this was that my STD test came back negative. I'm glad that nigga wasn't going around raping women and had an STD. Shoot, that nigga did do twenty years, there's no telling what went down up in that prison.

I was not fully over what happened to me because of Mace, but I was tired of lying in that bed day in and day out. Raydon had been on me and there for me every step of the way. I loved him even more for that.

I rinsed the soap off my body before turning the water off and stepping out of the shower. I stepped into the room, and Raydon was sitting on the side of the bed smoking, releasing a cloud of smoke from the blunt he was smoking. I swear this man was so sexy, sitting here in just a pair of boxer briefs. I was sure all thirty-two teeth were showing because my cheeks were definitely hurting from being stretched out.

I grabbed my lotion and applied it to my body. I could see him staring at me from the corner of my eye.

"I'm glad you getting out of here," Raydon said as he took the lotion from me and started doing what I was doing. I hadn't had sex with Raydon since the incident. For one, I wasn't comfortable, and two, I wanted to at least make sure I was clean first. He was being really patient with me, which was bringing me even closer to him.

I wasn't even mad at him about committing anymore because he had shown me how much he really cared. This nigga had love for my ass; he just wanted his cake and eat it too. Well, it wouldn't be any more eating cake unless it was mine.

"Yeah, it's time. I don't want to let what happened control me. Plus, you have helped a lot." I placed my hand on top of his, making him stop his hand movements.

I saw a hint of sadness come over him. I hadn't seen this look besides the night he found me.

"I thought I was going to lose you, Destiny. For real, girl, you are the only positive thing that holds steady in my life. You make sure I'm straight and even tell me when I'm wrong. I admire your drive and tenacity. You make my ass better, and that's a quality any nigga would want in a female; a quality that I want in mine. I am done, Destiny; I promise it's me and you."

"By this time, the tears were pouring down my face. Raydon even had a tear or two fall from his eyes, which was why I believed every word that he was saying. It was going to be me and him, and that's all I'd been wanting.

Eden

"Girl, I am so glad that you came out with me, girl," I said to Destiny, who was on the passenger side of my BMW.

I placed my hand on top of hers and gave it a light squeeze. This was her first time seeing it, and she flipped out, wanting Raydon to buy her one. Of course, I knew he was going to get her one, but she didn't know it. Reeno was pillow talking and told me.

"Yeah, it was time. I'm still torn about it, but I can't let what he did ruin my life. I know that Raydon is going to find him and put him out of his misery, and that's all that matters to me."

I nodded and continued to head to the nail salon, thinking about what she said. Mace was dead from what she told me, and Beast wasn't there at the time. Who would have ever thought that little ol' me would be OK with my nigga killing someone? This was different though, he hurt my cousin, so he needed to be dealt with.

"Come on, girl," I said once I was parked.

"How may we help you?" Chin Lee asked with his strong accent.

"Yes, we would both like pedicures and a gel fill-in," Destiny answered.

"You both come." Chin led us to the pedicure bowl where we both sat in the leather massage chair once we pulled off our flip-flops and sat them beside our chair.

The first thing I did was grab the remote control that controlled my chair. I had to get a steady rhythm going on my back, and it looked as if Destiny was going to do the same thing.

"So, what's up with you and Raydon now?" I asked as I placed my feet inside the half-filled tub.

Destiny smiled brightly. It was the first time that I have seen that smile.

"He has been acting differently since that day. He has been making all types of promises, but we will see."

"Promises like what, Destiny?"

"Well, he keeps saying that it's just me and him, and he wants to marry me."

"Awww, he really thought he was going to lose you. You should have seen him when I was telling him what was going on. But let's not talk about it anymore. Just don't give him a hard time."

"Yeah. I hear you."

We sat for a few minutes while we were getting our pedis. Destiny and I both looked up when we heard a woman say Reeno's name. She was on the phone and obviously upset that he wasn't picking up the phone for her.

"You hear this, cuzo?"

"Yeah, I hear it." I contemplated going over to the woman and seeing why she was talking about my man, but that wouldn't solve anything. I picked up my phone instead, sending a text message.

"Damn, he still not picking up. I have to get this right, or Beast will be mad at me."

This bitch tried to whisper, but I heard what she said, and I was now boiling inside. I looked over to Destiny and noticed she heard it too. I picked up my phone, sending another text. We just sat and listened to this bitch implementing herself in a damn crime.

I couldn't take it anymore; fuck not wanting to have drama in my life. I felt like heat was coursing through my body looking over wide-eyed at this hoe. This bitch was part of the problem. She was part of the plan that caused Destiny to get raped. She was part of the reason why my man was in the shit that he was in. This bitch diverted her eyes to me, causing me to sneer my nose up at her.

"What the fuck you looking at?" she asked me.

"For one, you over there talking about setting my man up. We don't play that shit over here." I let her know.

Destiny was already getting up out of her seat. Seeing her prompted me to get up too.

"Bitch, Reeno don't even have girlfriends, so I know for a fact you lying. I've been trying to secure him for a year now. Oh wait, you the same hoe from Terrace. Fuck you, bitch. I owe you one. She looked toward her friend with her scraggly ass hair, and they both laughed. Standing up, they walked toward us.

Destiny and I made our way toward them, but before we could reach them, the door chimed, and in strode Reeno with his brother. Reeno looked sexy as fuck coming in here to handle business. I glanced over at the girl as her smirk faded upon seeing Reeno come through the door walking straight to me and Raydon.

"What's up, Chin Lee," Reeno and Raydon both spoke before shaking his hand.

"I came to pay for my girl's shit," I heard Reeno say before reaching me, bending down to give me a passionate kiss. He knew exactly what he was doing.

All of a sudden, we heard a commotion by the door. Apparently, ol' girl realized she fucked up. She tried to run out but was caught by Zack outside the door.

I saw Raydon to tell Chin Lee something as Chin Lee discreetly got everyone out of the shop except the two girls that were talking. Next, I saw two white boys walk through the door bringing the two girls back inside, and then locked the door.

Ol' girl looked around, confused, and then looked back at Reeno.

"I'll be right back, baby."

Reeno then turned toward the girl and said, "So, your ass was in this shit to set me up? You were only fucking me in hopes of your boy catching me slippin'?"

Her friend was just standing there with her eyes wide open, while ol' girl, whose name I remembered was NaToya, didn't know what to say.

"Bitch, where the fuck is that nigga, Beast?" I heard Raydon scream.

His ass made me jump a little bit. I didn't know what the guys were going to do to this NaToya bitch and her friend, but I would hate to be on the receiving end of it.

"Reeno, please, I had no choice," her voice quavered as she tried to speak.

"Nah, bitch, you were going to get me killed. Plus, that fuck nigga raped my sister. Fuck you, NaToya."

He nodded toward the two white guys who dragged NaToya out of the nail salon but kept her quivering friend. Reeno walked up close to her and asked, "What you see?"

She immediately began shaking her head. I could tell she was terrified. Reeno grabbed her purse, throwing it to Raydon who pulled her license out of it.

"Davis Lake Dr.," Raydon recited as he threw her pocketbook back to her, minus her wallet.

"Now I know where you live. If I hear anything, I know where to come. Don't fuck with me. Let her go."

She was pushed toward the door where she fell and scrambled to stand before bolting to the door to leave. I swear, seeing Reeno in action had me hot as fuck. He strode over to me, pulling me and then looked up at Chin. Reeno pulled a big stack of money out of his pocket, peeled off ten one-hundred-dollar bills, and handed them over to Chin, letting him know it was for the customers that he had to miss out on for shutting down the shop.

I grabbed ahold of his arm and stood on my tippy toes so that he could hear what I was saying, "That shit turned my ass on, baby."

"Oh, yeah. I will handle that pussy after I handle this business." He then kissed me and was out the door.

Chapter 22

Raydon

Before we did anything else, we needed to get to the spot where Zack took NaToya so that we could find out where this dumb ass nigga was. I didn't like the way my baby was crying in the nail salon from hearing what NaToya was saying. I'm sure that if we wouldn't have walked in when we did, Destiny would have whipped that hoe's ass.

I couldn't believe that Beast sent her ass at my brother, but what I'm most worried about is, why my brother didn't see that shit coming.

"Bruh, what the fuck?" I asked before taking a long pull of the blunt I had just rolled.

I needed this shit from finding out the lengths this nigga had went through to try and get to us all because of some old shit.

"I don't even know, Raydon. She didn't show any signs. I keep running shit through my mind and can't think of anything that she did that would make me think that she was up to no good. I mean, this bitch been around way before that nigga got out."

I passed his ass the blunt, and he took it. Shit, apparently, he needed it too. We drove in silence the rest of the way in our own thoughts. Before I knew it, I was pulling up to the house off Boswell Rd.

"What's the end result?" I questioned him before we got out of the car.

We didn't normally handle females, but this situation was different. She violated in the worst way. She was helping get us killed, and since it was Reeno who she was running game on, he would be the one to make the decision. He knew that I was down for whatever.

"We do what we need to do to make her give up that info. If she has to be tortured to death, then that's what it is."

I nodded in understanding as we headed to the back door. We walked in to see Warren sitting in front of NaToya with a bat in his hand. He was the warm-up, but we were there now.

"Appreciate that, bro, but we got it from here."

"No problem. Her ass tryna be tough, but I know y'all can break her."

"Fa'sho," I responded to him.

NaToya sat with her eyes drooped and blood running down her mouth like Warren had to smack her ass. Her eyes followed Reeno to the table that Warren had set up for us. Then her eyes diverted to Zack and Chad. We had them wait around just in case. We didn't know how this was going to go.

"You ready to talk now, love?" Reeno squatted in front of her trembling body. Baby girl was scared, and I didn't understand why she wouldn't give the mothafucka up.

"Your life depends on this. Where is that raping bastard at?" I asked.

"I can't. He will kill me."

The sadistic laughter coming from my brother's mouth would have made me worry if I wasn't used to the shit. His hand found its way to the side of her face. He stroked it softly, then drew back and let loose, smacking the fuck out of her.

"Got daaaamn!" Zack yelled while Chad chuckled.

"If you don't, *you will* be dead."

Reeno waited for a second, and when she didn't say anything, he took the same metal bat that Warren had, swung it twice, cracking both of her kneecaps. He then threw the bat down and turned toward me to say, "Untie her."

"Ahhhhh! Noooooo!" NaToya continued to scream after what she had gotten herself into resonated through her brain.

Reeno picked up a pair of wire cutters he had laid out on the floor. This was the part of my brother that many didn't know about. They knew he didn't take any shit, but this was on a whole other level. The deranged look in his eyes when he wanted something had anyone he crossed regretting it until they didn't even care to die. His victims would often rather welcome death than to deal with his psycho ass. He showed no amount of remorse as he yanked her right hand, holding it down on the edge of the chair with her fingers hanging off the edge.

"Now, where is he?" My brother asked once again. It wasn't going to be too many more times that he would ask. I just sat my ass on the end of the table, waiting.

She looked up at him with tears streaming down her face mixed with blood.

"I wasn't going to tell him anything," her ass tried to lie.

SNIP.

"Ahhhhhhhhhh!"

SNIP.

"Ahhhhhhhhhhh!"

SNIP. Crack."

That was the third finger Reeno cut off. He had nothing else to say. I then grabbed a lighter and held it against each finger that he amputated. He then cut the other two and I burnt those. By this time, NaToya had passed out.

"A, bring a bucket of water and throw it on this bitch." I looked behind me, telling one of the guys.

She struggled to breathe once the water was thrown on her.

"Just kill me please," she stated.

Instead of responding, two fingers from her other hand were cut off at the knuckle. But this time, once her piercing scream moved through the air, she gave up.

"OK, OK, I will tell you," she said as her head came up from her chest. You could tell she was in a lot of pain, but you could also see that she was about to say some shit we didn't want to hear.

I stood up, walking next to my brother as she rattled off an address.

"But he's not there; you better get to your parents' house." She laughed as best she could.

"What the fuck you say, bitch?" Reeno asked as he continuously punched this bitch out.

"Reeno, stop. You heard her. We have to go. Just kill the bitch and let's go."

He stopped, pulling out his gun, shooting her right between the eyes.

"Y'all handle this and meet us at my parents' house." I turned to Zach and Chad, and then turned to Warren and said, "You come with us." Everybody sprang into action. It was a race against time to save my parents.

Reeno

"Fuuuccccckkkkk! Drive this bitch, bruh!" I screamed as loud as I could. I wasn't upset with Raydon or anything, I just needed to get to my parents.

I looked down at my vibrating phone, noticing it was Eden. I was supposed to come home to her, but this shit has taken a turn. I attempted to calm my nerves before answering the call.

"What's up, Ms. Eden. It's not a good time."

"Hey, you're not here, and I was beginning to worry."

"Yeah, something else came up." I sighed.

"Is everything OK?"

"Honestly no, but it's nothing for you to worry about."

The line was quiet for a minute before she said, "Come back to me. Whatever you do, just come back to me."

I felt that shit in my heart, which further let me know what I'd been feeling was real.

"E, I will always come back to the woman I love."

All of a sudden, the car swerved into the other lane, causing me to look over at my brother, who despite the situation, had a goofy grin on his face.

"What the fuck, nigga. Pay attention to the fucking road."

"Cupcakin' ass nigga." Was all he said as he pulled onto our parents' street. This was the longest thirty minutes of my life.

"Reeno, Reeno."

"I'm here, baby. But listen, I meant what I said. I have to go now."

"OK, baby, and I heard you. I am going to stay home until I hear from you. I love you too. Just come back."

With that said, we ended the call. Warren passed us our weapons before the three of us filed out of the truck. We didn't have a plan; our only objective was to save my fucking parents. I wanted to know how this fool got up in here anyway. My parent's security system was supposed to be top of the line. For real, if something happened to them, I was going up in that building and shootin' that shit up.

As we walked up the driveway and into the backyard, I observed my surroundings and the movement that I could see inside the house, which wasn't a lot because the lights were dim.

I turned the knob to the back door, and it was already unlocked. I heard whimpering coming from the front room. Figuring it was my mother, I made my way toward the front, holding my finger to my lips, informing them to make as little noise as possible. I got to the end of the hall, and Raydon crossed to the other side.

"You thought you could ruin my life and the shit be OK, but now that I'm about to get some of this pretty pussy. You over here begging," we heard Beast say. Me and my brother glanced at each other, and before I could say anything, he ran out screaming with his gun pointed. All I saw was Beast raise his gun as I hurriedly ran out in front of my brother, jumping in front of him and letting off a shot. I hit the ground and looked up at Warren kicking Beast's gun away. I watched my brother stand frozen until he snapped out of it, moving toward my half-naked mother.

Raydon untied her as Warren untied my father. That's when I felt a stinging sensation.

"Oh my god, baby."

My mother rushed over to me with a blanket wrapped around her with tears still running down her cheeks. This nigga was really going to rape my mother. I felt the frown on my face, not even caring that I was bleeding. At that moment, I had all the strength in the world as I stood, bypassed my mother, and rushed over to Beast, yanking him up and placing my arm around his neck.

"You were going to rape my mother, you bitch ass nigga. First, you come for my sis, now my heart. Die, nigga."

I squeezed tighter while this big, black, monkey looking nigga struggled. He tried to pry my arm from around him, but nah, that shit wasn't happening. Finally, his arms dropped to his side like dead weight, and at that point, I dropped him.

My head turned toward my mother, who was being held by my father. My brother was sitting on the couch with his head in his hands. I knew what he was thinking, but I needed him to take me to E.

"Ma, I'm sorry."

She glanced over at my brother and already knew that I wanted to leave. She nodded, walking over to me, tying a shirt around my arm.

"I got this around here, son." Stanford glanced up just as Zack and Chad came through the door.

"Bruh."

Raydon pulled his head up, turning toward me with his red eyes and not saying a word.

"I need to go get my arm fixed bruh. I will call E and tell them we on the way. You call Doc to meet us."

He finally stood up, headed toward me. I was getting weaker by the minute. I just couldn't give up. Raydon placed his hand around my shoulder and whispered, "Sorry, bro."

"I'm going to be good." I responded. I then looked back at my father, "Take care of my momma. We'll be back."

When my father agreed, we left out, leaving them to handle Beast's body and my father to make sure my mother was all right. Right now, I needed to get this shoulder sewed up, it hurt like a mothafucka.

Chapter 23

Destiny

I was suddenly awakened by loud banging on my door. I sat up and listened to make sure I wasn't dreaming or anything, but when Eden made her way into my room, I knew I wasn't tripping. She walked over to my window to look outside and then bolted out the room, saying that it was Reeno's car. Immediately, I assumed something was wrong, so I jumped up too. I damn near jumped down four steps at a time to get to the bottom.

This time, someone was kicking the door. I pulled the door open to see a puddle of blood underneath Reeno and Raydon, and Raydon was holding a weakened Reeno.

"No, no, no, no, no, oh my God. No, no, no." Eden stood there with her eyes wide and hands covering her mouth with tears in her eyes.

"Baby girl." Reeno reached for her with his right arm as soon as Raydon helped him through the door.

Raydon helped him to the kitchen chair as he said to Eden, "Calm down, baby. I'm here, and I need your help. Be down for me right now. I came here just in case I had to speak to you if it was going to be my last. I just need you to help clean it." He pulled her down with his good arm and kissed her lips.

She nodded as Raydon told me to go get my first aid kit, peroxide, whatever I had. I held it together the best I could for Eden and Raydon and did as he asked. Once I got back, we cleaned our hands and then used wet rags and antiseptic wash to clean around the wound.

Eden then straddled Reeno's lap and poured peroxide on the wound. I could tell it hurt by the way Reeno screamed.

"Our boy will be here to stitch him up in a little bit. I just wanted to start cleaning it and applying pressure to stop the bleeding."

Right when Raydon said that, there was a knock at the door. He went to answer it, and true enough, a tall, lanky black guy greeted me and walked through the door with his medical bag. This was insane; they had an answer to everything.

"What's up, doc?" They both spoke to who I now knew was Dr. Henry.

He immediately got to work on Reeno by first giving him a few pills for pain, and then he handed Raydon some extras if he needed them later.

Twenty minutes later, Reeno was stitched up, patched up, and given instructions for the next few days. Once the doctor left, Eden helped Reeno to her room, while me and Raydon stayed downstairs to clean up the droplets of blood all over the floor and outside before it dried too bad.

Finally finishing an hour later, we took a shower and were finally in bed.

"Raydon, what happened?" I asked because I could tell something was bothering him.

After what felt like forever, he answered with, "Ol' girl told us Beast was at our parents' house, and when we got there, I froze up seeing that mothafucka about to rape my mother with my father tied up, not being able to do shit. Reeno took that bullet for me. What if it would have been worse? What if he would have died? I can't live without my brother."

I immediately started shaking my head. "Reeno did that because he loves you. He saw you were in trouble and did what he felt was right with you being his little brother."

"I know, but…"

"No buts, Raydon. He is OK, baby, and you are OK." I rubbed his back. He was really down about this, but it was OK because I was going to be there for him like he was there for me. He said I made him better, and this situation was no different. I'm just glad everyone was OK.

Eden

I unwrapped the plastic bag from around Reeno's wound once we were out of the shower. I checked his shoulder to be sure that his bandage was still dry and clean. I then helped him into a pair of boxers before I dressed in my nightgown.

Reeno laid on his back as I laid on his right side with my right leg draped over his thigh. My hand landed on his abs as I used my fingertips to trace each one.

"What you thinking about, E?"

I heard his scruffy voice ask me. I kissed his shoulder before I responded, "How I thought I would lose you. All of that blood… I guess it looked worse than what it was."

He lifted his good arm and allowed me to move closer before letting his arm drop around me.

"I made a promise to you, and no bullet was going to stop me from fulfilling that shit."

I reached up, allowing my face to get close to his before I let my tongue roam around in his mouth before straddling him, and causing him to hiss when my head accidentally hit his hurt shoulder. "Oooh, I'm so sorry, maybe I should stay over here," I said while preparing myself to move back to my previous spot beside him.

Reeno hurriedly grabbed my waist with his right hand and assured me that he was OK.

"Nah, stay your ass up here. I feel that warmness between your legs. I'm not against you handlin' this."

He pointed to his rock-hard dick, licking his lips. He lifted my nightgown and then peered back up at me with his eyebrow raised. I giggled because I knew what he was saying before he said it.

"Girl, you knew what your ass was doing."

His smile was so sexy to me. When that mole lifted with his cheeks, it made me want to bite it off. Nasty, I know.

I slid his boxers down with him helping by lifting his ass up. Placing my knees on the bed, my hand circled around his dick before I circled his head with my tongue and then gathered enough saliva in my mouth before letting it flow onto his hardened dick.

I devoured all ten and a half inches once I relaxed my throat. My head bounced up and down with his hand running through my hair. I didn't think he knew what to do with me at times. I gave that fire head, and I knew it by the way his eyes were closed tightly, his teeth bearing down on his lips, and the way his toes were curling when I came up for air to look. His cum sprayed down my throat once he couldn't take anymore.

"I swear you're going to have a nigga marrying yo' ass sooner than later."

All I could do was blush as I took hold of his dick, placing it at my entrance. I eased down before getting into a slow wind, twirling my hips back and forth. I closed my eyes for a few seconds as the euphoric feeling of his dick coursed through my body. I felt that shit from my throat to the tip of my big toe. I moaned as I gently placed my hands on his abs to help steady myself.

"Fuck, E." I watched him watch me with his bottom lip between his teeth.

"Mmmmm, damn, I love this dick." I bent down, continuing to bounce my ass as my lips found his.

I sped up my pace, and he met me thrust for thrust. I could have sworn I was in heaven. Before I knew it, we were both exploding. I laid right there on top of him until I caught my breath. Then I cleaned us both up so that we could lay back down.

Silence filled the room around us until he spoke. "I appreciate you helping me out today, E. You were able to push your feelings aside for a minute until you got me cleaned up. I love that shit. You could have folded, but you didn't. I know your little ass not used to this life, but the two times something happened, you did as I asked and handled it well."

I had grown to love this man with everything in me during the short time that we'd been acquainted. I was worried when we first started talking and things weren't going well, but that had all changed now. Now I don't think I could be without him. Hopefully, things stayed this way.

Stanford

Thank God things were finally settled down in my house. I would have died if something happened to my wife. Knowing that deranged mothafucka was out there, I knew better than to step outside at night to smoke. I could have gone right on down to my man cave or any of the other five spare bedrooms we had.

That's how he got in. It's like he was waiting on me to come out. He must have been watching me because I did that almost every night. I must be getting old as fuck because that shit wouldn't have happened a few years ago. The guys handled that bitch nigga and cleaned up. It was like nothing ever happened. I'm just glad, however, that my boys found out when they did.

Zack and Chad handled Beast's body with the help of Warren, and then we all kind of cleaned up the fucking blood that was on my walls and floors. After letting them out of the house and setting the alarm, I headed upstairs to find my wife in the tub.

I stripped down and got in the shower next to her. Once finished, I dried off and put on a pair of boxer briefs. I then kneeled down on the floor, grabbed her rag, and began washing her off. I washed every crack and crevice of her body before she allowed me to lift her up and carry her to the bed. I made sure to dry her body off and apply lotion before I flipped the switch to turn the lights off and get in the bed.

"I'm so sorry, baby. I messed up. I wasn't paying attention to my surroundings, and that man hurt you. It could have been worse."

"You are right, it could have been worse, but it wasn't. I'm OK, and that's all that matter."

Leena grabbed my hand, holding it in her own. Her beautiful brown eyes ogled mine, letting me know she wasn't mad at all.

"It's just, if something would have happened to you, I probably would have died."

A tear slipped from my eye, followed by more. I could not stop them as I thought about my wife being dead or even raped. She pulled me to the top of her and said, "Baby, I'm here, and you're here. We are alright. You feel this?"

Her hand went into my boxers, pulling out my shit and guiding me to her tight pussy. My wife may be in her late forties, but she knew how to work that pussy. She knew exactly what her husband needed. My tears dried up quick, feeling her warmness surround my dick. I took my time with her, making love until we both let loose.

"I love how you still gangsta with it, Stan. I know you would have done anything to prevent him from hurting me."

Damn, my dick was back hard just like that. I loved it when my wife tugged at my ego. I guess her ass was about to get this daddy dick now.

■ ■

My phone kept blaring in my ear; I wanted to throw that shit out the window. Me and my wife was already up all night. Yeah, we knew how to put it down in the bedroom, but we were not young anymore.

"Hello."

"What up, pops?" my son responded.

"Nothing, son. Everything is fine. Me and yo' momma had a nice workout last night."

"Stan."

"Dad."

My wife and son said at the same time. I chuckled at their antics. Both of them knew what it was.

"Me and Raydon wanted to make sure things were OK, but I can see that it is."

"Yes, it is."

"Tell him and his brother to bring their women to dinner Sunday. I'm not playing."

"You heard your mother, son."

"Yes, I heard her. I will tell everyone."

"OK, son, we are going back to sleep. Later."

"Later."

I grabbed my wife and held her tight. We definitely needed a little more rest and were about to get it. These were the moments that I treasured with Leena the most. Just me and her, holding each other, lying in bed with our skin touching.

Chapter 24

Raydon

Sunday Evening

"My momma already warned that if we weren't there then she would come looking for you and Eden."

"What!"

Destiny yelped with her eyes stretched wider than I've ever seen them shits. I chortled just watching before I said, "It will be OK. My mother is the nicest woman you will ever meet, and my father is cool as fuck. I mean, I was made from his mold, so you know he cool."

Destiny's head fell back while she laughed at my ass and said, "Conceited much?"

"Nah, baby, I'm just confident in myself."

"If you say so. But how is my outfit? It's not too revealing is it?"

"Woman, you look perfect to me."

"Raydon..." She stomped her foot down on the ground and continued to say, "But is it *meet the parents* perfect?"

"Look..." I grabbed both of her shoulders. "You look fine, and my parents will love you just like I do. I don't even know why you're worried. You have on jeans and a nice top."

"Yeah, but my cleavage is showing."

"That may be, Destiny, but those big ol' things will show either way."

We both laughed, and she hit my ass. It's cool though, at least she was straight now. I went ahead and grabbed my keys and the other things I needed before we headed outside to pull my Porsche out of the garage and head to my parents' home.

"You ready for this, babe?" I turned in my seat to ask Destiny when we pulled up to my parents' house. She wasn't paying attention to me though, because she was too busy admiring the house.

"Destiny?"

"Oh, sorry. This house's details are just so immaculate. But yes, I am as ready as I could be."

"Good."

Reeno and Eden pulled up as soon as I shut my door, and I was rounding the car to let Destiny out.

"Bro, her ass scared, ain't she?" I asked Reeno, who started laughing like hell.

"Fuck yeah. Her ass was worried about her clothes and shit. I was like, 'look, don't worry about all of that, and our parents don't care.'"

"I told Destiny the same shit," I let Reeno know.

"We are standing right here you know." They chimed in simultaneously.

Reeno and I couldn't help but burst into laughter as we grabbed their hands, escorting them to the front door. I lifted my hand to unlock the door before stepping inside our parents' home.

"Maaaaa!" Reeno yelled, even though he knew our mother didn't like that shit. She'd rather you come find her, which judging by the aroma of her bomb ass cooking, she was in the kitchen. I headed that way, but she was already walking down the hallway covered in an apron with a big ass spoon in her hand. My mother was gorgeous. Her skin was glowing, and although she was dressed down, she was still beautiful.

"Boy, if I wasn't cooking with this spoon, I'd smack you with it." My mother smirked before hugging and kissing the both of us.

"You going to hit me with my arm in a sling?" Reeno asked.

"And I would still love you."

"I love you too, ma." Reeno hugged her back. "But this house too damn big to come looking for you." He kissed her cheek.

"Ma, this is my woman, Eden, by the way." He introduced them. My brother was really feeling Eden, and I was happy for him. At least he didn't have to deal with psycho ass bitches anymore.

"You are so gorgeous. Both of you are, not that I expect anything less from my boys though." She hugged Eden.

"It's a pleasure, Mrs. Brooks," Eden responded.

And then my mother turned toward me to introduce my girl.

"Ma, this is my lady, Destiny."

"Nice to meet you, Destiny," she said, hugging her.

"Nice to meet you too, Mrs. Brooks." Destiny smiled pleasantly.

"OK, now that introductions are out the way, you two come with me to the kitchen so we can chat. Reeno and Raydon, your father wants to talk to you before dinner. He's downstairs."

"Yes, ma'am," we answered.

I felt Destiny's hand tighten around mine. I pulled her close and whispered in her ear, "It's OK."

"Sweetie, I don't bite. Come on." My mother grabbed her hand, and the three of them walked down the hall toward the kitchen.

Me and my brother took the stairs to my father's man cave. He was sitting on the couch, smoking a cigar, and watching the newest episode of *Power*.

"Hey, sons. Grab you a drink. I'm watching the last ten minutes, and I will be finished," he spoke without looking up at us.

"A'ight." We went to his bar in the corner of the room and then took a seat.

I swear everybody watched this show. I liked to watch it at its original time though. When the credits started rolling, he got to the reason he needed to talk to us.

"So, after the fiasco, did y'all take precautions?" Stan looked between the two of us with raised brows.

"Yeah, pops. We changed two houses and switched the times, plus locations, of all drops down to the day. We also moved everything out of the warehouse." Reeno let him know.

"That's good. OK, let's go meet these ladies of yours."

Back upstairs in the kitchen, my mom and our women were laughing and enjoying themselves. I introduced my father to the girls, and after he held a conversation with each of them, he discreetly gave his approval. This was the shit I loved. Everyone that truly mattered in the same room. Not to mention, Leena threw down in the kitchen. Salad, BBQ chicken, mac and cheese, fried chicken, cabbage, and rice. A nigga was full. Now I was ready to go home and fuck the shit out of my girl.

Chapter 25

Reeno

That next Saturday

"Damn you look fine as fuck, baby." I stood behind Eden, who was in the mirror doing some shit to her hair.

She was wearing the fuck out of the dress she had on. It wasn't tight, but it was short as shit and turning me on. I kissed her neck as my hand traveled up her thighs.

"Stop, babe." She giggled and then said, "You're going to mess up my outfit." I didn't care nothing about what she was saying. My belt was already being unbuckled and my pants were hitting the floor. I had to be careful with my arm, but I was getting shit done.

"I have to, or I'm going to have a hard dick all night. I will be quick, and I won't mess anything up.

"Shit." Her body shuddered as my middle finger swirled around her clit. I knew for a fact she would have to change her panties.

"Won't we be late for our reservations?" she inquired. I couldn't let her know that we really didn't have reservations, so I pulled her panties down to her feet so that she could step out of them. I then lifted her dress to her waist, positioning my head at her opening and easing my way in. We both let out a satisfied moan as I pumped in and out of her. She moaned so loud, I didn't know what to do but pound in and out of her harder, causing her to scream.

"Yes, fuck me. Get it, baby."

"Fuck me back." I smacked her right cheek hard as fuck, causing her to do as I said. Baby girl was going as hard as me.

The curve in my dick kept hitting her spot, making her shit wet as fuck. After a few more strokes, she screamed, and I growled, exploding inside of her, not even caring what would happen. I stayed inside her until I felt as if my nuts were empty and then slowly pulled out.

"Get undressed. Let's take a quick shower."

******

"Aren't we going the wrong way?" Eden asked as we drove to our destination.

"No, I have to stop by the club real quick. It won't take long."

Eden gave me the side-eye like she didn't believe me. I chuckled at her little ass.

Ten minutes later, we were at the club. I asked her to come in with me real quick, and she followed along. I had let Raydon know we were pulling up, so everyone could be in position. When we first walked through the doors, it was pitch black. You couldn't see anything.

"Y'all closed today or something?" she asked.

"Nah." I flipped the lights on, and that's when everybody screamed,

"Surprise!"

"Oh my God." She looked around wide-eyed with her hand covering her mouth. Some of the people she knew, others were just there for their regular night of fun but agreed to participate in the surprise.

I looked around and met eyes with A'Myracle. She didn't look happy at all, but I wasn't worried about her right now, and I hope she didn't pick tonight to fuck with me. Tonight was about E.

"Happy Birthday, cuz." Destiny gave her a hug.

A few girls that Eden went to school with came down to party with her. The look on her face let me know that she was both shocked and excited. A nigga did good.

I had the girls decorate the place fit for a queen. I even had a special chair in VIP for her. It was gold and big, just for my lady. I led the way to the section that we were all in as the DJ dropped the beat.

"Hey, hey, hey." Eden danced in her chair to Cardi B.

"What's up, bruh. You look debonair today." Raydon bumped fists with me.

My mom and pops stepped into VIP, showing Eden love.

"Thanks, Mr. and Mrs. Brooks. I appreciate you being here."

"Of course, baby, but we're not staying. We will leave the partying to the young folks." My mom answered. Her and my pops said good-bye and left the club.

"Babe, I got you a dance."

Eden wasn't used to things like this, but I planned on turning her out tonight for her twenty-fourth birthday.

Sinful Bliss walked into VIP wearing nothing but a thong and pasties. Eden's mouth dropped to the floor as she looked over at me and swallowed.

"Enjoy, baby." I handed her a stack of singles just as Rihanna's *Throw It Up*, could be heard throughout the club.

This bitch Sinful Bliss was gettin' it. She was poppin' her ass in Eden's lap, and Eden was droppin' ones on her ass. When Eden smacked her on her ass, I knew she was feeling it. I filled her another shot and handed it to her. She downed it immediately. She stood up and danced with Sinful Bliss. It was a sight to see.

We were all having a good time until A'Myracle got on stage. I didn't know what she was planning, but something told me the shit wasn't going to be pretty. I turned toward Raydon, and he knew I wanted him to go yank her ass down. I was already pissed because I knew whatever she was going to say was some bullshit.

I noticed a box type thing in her hand as she eyed me. I eyed her ass back, letting her know not to play with me. She pressed a button in her hand and pink and blue balloons fell from high in the ceiling. I didn't even notice that shit before. I mean, who would look high up in the fucking ceiling. This bitch had me fucked up.

I played it cool though because I didn't want to look guilty, which I wasn't. A banner that said, congratulations to my baby daddy, Reeno was also displayed against the wall beside the stage. When the fuck did this bitch get to do all this shit? The DJ stopped the music and turned toward me. I shook my shoulders because I didn't know what the fuck she was talking about.

"Ladies and gentlemen, I would like to announce my pregnancy. My child's father Ree…"

Everybody in the club gasped. There were whispers and people pointing. It was crazy as fuck.

"Pregnant?" Eden whispered to herself.

No this bitch didn't, I thought to myself

A'Myracle didn't get to say anything else because Raydon grabbed her by her arm and yanked her ass off the stage, dragging her to the back stairs. The fact that she took her time and did all of this shit, let me know that her ass was crazy.

"Get off of me, Raydon. I hate him. His ass knew I should have been the one. But no, he want to get this skinny bitch!" A'Myracle screamed.

"What the fuck?" I heard Eden yell this time as she glared down at me.

"It's not true, baby. I promise, I haven't touched that girl since me and you. She is delusional as fuck, baby," I pleaded.

Eden wasn't the type to cause a scene, so she stood and stormed out, and I jumped up to go after her, but Destiny stopped me and said, "Handle your business with that hoe. I got my cousin. I knew that girl was crazy from the start. Don't worry."

"Well, I wish you would have told me." I pointed to the DJ for him to turn the music back on. I walked over to Sinful Bliss and said, "I will pay you if you get dressed and go across the street to get a pregnancy test. This bitch about to prove this shit."

"No, Reeno, you don't have to pay me. You paid enough for tonight, but I will run over there really quick."

"I appreciate that," I said as I headed downstairs to where I knew Raydon had taken the bitch.

Her ass was sitting on the couch crying. I didn't know what for, but we damn sure were getting to the bottom of this. I took a chair from in front of the desk and sat it in front of her before sitting down. My brother was sitting on the couch to the right of her, equally as mad.

"What's the problem, A'Myracle? Why did you do this lame ass shit?"

She sniffed, wiping her eyes and shit, putting on a show before saying, "I tried to talk to you this whole time, and you pushed me away. I should have been next in line."

"What the fuck you think he is, A? Ain't no fuckin' line to get to him. If he found what he really wanted, then he just found that shit," Raydon blurted. He wasn't with this shit either, I already knew she was unemployed.

"But he was mine first."

"He was mine first," I mocked. "You sound like a child."

I got a text from outside the door, which I asked Raydon to get. When he returned, he handed me two boxes of pregnancy tests. I opened one box, handing it to her. Her eyes showed fear. That's when I grinned because I knew I had her ass.

"What do you want me to do with that?"

"It's a pregnancy text, girl, what you think? Now, get your ass up and go to that bathroom." I stood, getting in her face, causing her to cry harder as she grabbed the test and went into the bathroom.

"Damn, bruh. I thought we got rid of all the crazy," Raydon spoke up.

"This hoe is out of her mind. I'm glad I got Eden. Well, after this, I don't know, bruh."

"Man, you know she lying. I know you were fucking with her heavy at one point, but she knows her ass not pregnant." We both agreed just as she exited the bathroom with the test in her hand.

When she handed to me and I looked down at it, I lifted my hand and smacked the shit out of her. I mean, I didn't mean to smack her that hard. That was a pimp slap. Her ass landed on the floor.

"Daaaaamn!" My brother was laughing so hard he was holding his stomach.

I kneeled down in front of her and squeezed her chin, saying, "You have two choices. I kill you right now for lying to me, or you leave and never return because you know your ass is out of a fuckin' job now, hoe." I knocked her head back, making it bounce off the floor.

"What the fuck were you thinking, A? You thought he wasn't going to check that shit?" Raydon said what he had to say.

"I, I will leave since I don't have a job anymore." She sat up with her feet planted on the floor and her knees to her chest. Her weave was all over the place, and her mascara was running down her face.

"You may as well dry your fuckin' face. You ruined my girl's night, and for what? I still don't want your ass. Even if you were pregnant, I still wouldn't be with your ass. Me and my girl would have worked that shit out. Now get the fuck out of my establishment!" I bellowed.

She hurriedly stood and ran out the back door. She knew what it was. She didn't want to risk suffering the consequences. The only reason I let her go was because she was cool peoples at one point. Now all I needed to do was go chase my girl down. I just hoped she was willing to listen.

Eden

I hadn't spoken to Reeno since the incident at the club two nights ago. He has tried to call, text, and even find me, but I just needed a minute. I always knew it was going to be some shit with that girl.

I understood what Destiny was saying about that crazy girl, but I wanted to be sure. I couldn't stand her ass for ruining my birthday like that, and from what Destiny told me, the bitch was not even pregnant at all. What type of dumb bitch do you have to be to say you're pregnant, but you really not? Did the hoe think that he wasn't going to check or something?

I was just finishing up with my first day of class, which went great by the way. I was ecstatic about what was to come with my first year as a biology teacher at Independence High School. I was walking outside to my car, looking down at my phone until I ran into this hard body.

I looked up from my phone to see a large bouquet of flowers first, followed by Reeno's handsome face. Of course, he was dressed in a full tailored suit, looking good enough to devour at this very moment. I didn't act on it though. I just stood there stone-faced.

"What's up, baby. This is for you." His smile was so handsome. Oooh, I swear I hate him.

It was taking all of me not to just jump on this man right now. I hadn't seen this man in two days; he knew what his ass was doing.

"May I help you, Mr. Brooks?"

"Come on, E. That girl was lying, and I sent you a picture of the pregnancy test. I'm all about you, baby, and you know it."

I turned around and headed toward my car. Of course, he was behind me, pleading and calling my name. But I made him sweat until I opened my car door and placed my briefcase and purse inside. I then turned around with a bright smile on my face.

"Why you playin', man?" He chuckled. "Come here."

I walked closer to him, circling my arms around his neck, standing on my tippy toes and kissing his juicy lips. His hands fell to my ass as he squeezed a little.

"I missed you," I let him know.

"I missed your ass too. I swear I was going to find and kill that girl if you didn't come back to me."

"You love me that much, baby?" I asked.

"Fuck yeah. Follow me to the crib."

With that said, I hopped into my car and followed him to his house. I couldn't wait because I knew I was about to get it.

Chapter 26
Destiny

I turned to my left in order to get a good look at myself in the full-length mirror hanging on my bedroom wall. Damn, I looked good. I turned back around to make sure that my hair and makeup was OK, and I felt it was. I walked back into my bedroom to make sure everything I needed was packed.

With everything that Eden and I had been through these past few months with our men, we deserved this trip that Reeno and Raydon were sending us on; all-expense paid trip to New York City. I had to talk Eden into going. She was concerned about going on a trip so soon, but I finally was able to convince her. I mean, this was New York City, a place neither of us had ever been too.

Eden sat her luggage beside my bedroom and then asked, "You almost ready? We should be leaving soon to catch our flight." She sat on the edge of my bed and crossed her left leg over her right. I loved my cousin, she was always killing it. She was dressed in a pair of black joggers, a white off-the-shoulder crop top, same as me, and we would still turn heads.

"Yes, I just need to put my shoes on." I sat down on the bed next to Eden, reaching on the floor for my Vans and putting them on my feet. "OK, you need to stop, boo. If you're not, I'm ready for the both of us." I continued.

"I'm ready, Destiny. I just wish Reeno could make it."

Eden looked sad, and I felt bad for her. She would be OK though, especially when we got there. We would be having so much fun that she wouldn't even notice.

"Girl, we are going to have so much fun you won't even be thinking about him." I stood to reach for my purse and keys.

I could see Eden thinking about what I said before she responded with, "Yeah, you're right."

We both grabbed our luggage and was out the door to our awaiting town car to take us to Charlotte Douglas Airport.

******

We landed at John F. Kennedy Airport after being in the air for an hour and a half. We grabbed our bags and went outside to catch a cab. Our reservations were at The Ritz Carlton Central Park.

As soon as we walked into the hotel to check-in, we fell in love. Upon checking in, we realized that we had two suites. I wondered why we needed two rooms. We could have really slept in one room if you asked me.

"Girl, they showed out, didn't they?" I asked Eden.

"Hell yeah, they did."

My cousin was smiling from ear to ear just as I thought she would. Our rooms were right beside each other. We made plans to meet back up once we freshened up from being on the plane. Eden opened her door first, and I heard her scream.

"Oh my God! What is it?" I hurriedly opened my hotel room door to throw my things in, but when I did, I saw exactly why Eden was screaming.

I jumped up and down before dropping my bags and running toward Raydon, jumping into his arms. He was just standing there in a suit and tie, something that he preferred not to wear. He caught me, holding me tight while kissing all over my neck and face.

"I can't believe you are here. You tricked me."

"I know, baby. I had to surprise you though," he said before putting me down.

I admired the suite we were in. It was so big, and the view of central park was amazing. People looked like ants from how high up we were.

Raydon picked up my bags and brought them to the bedroom.

"Come on. We have dinner planned for y'all. Wear something sexy." He smacked my ass before going into the living room to wait on me to get dressed.

Me, Raydon, Eden, and Reeno sat in the back of our limo, waiting for the driver to come around and open the door. Once he did, I stepped out and observed the busy streets around me. The guys obviously had Imani Caribbean Kitchen and Bar in Brooklyn shut down. There was no one outside, and the restaurant looked deserted.

We walked into the place, and it was only us like I thought. We sat at a table in the middle of the restaurant. Eden and I were both all excited because we loved Caribbean food.

"We in Brooklyn now, baby!" Raydon shouted like he had issues, causing a ripple of laughter from everyone.

"Good evening, I will be your server. What will you all like to drink?"

The waitress came out, her accent heavy. We gave our drink and appetizer orders. When she stepped away, I watched as this fool demanded the attention of the others at the table. I mean, he didn't ask, he told them to shut the fuck up.

"How rude," Eden expressed while rolling her eyes.

"Didn't I tell you to shut up?"

I was waiting on Reeno to say something to Raydon for speaking to Eden that way, but he must have known his brother wasn't wrapped too tight. He just kissed Eden's neck and shook his head no.

"Yo, Destiny…" Raydon began to speak but never got it out because he dropped to his knees.

"Oh my God!" I started screaming and covered my mouth with my hand.

"What's wrong with you?" he asked me as he got back up off the floor. Just as I was about to get mad because I was embarrassed, he grabbed my hand.

"Let's go get married, girl."

I mean, it wasn't romantic or anything, but what do you expect from a street nigga?

"I mean, since you pretty much demanded and didn't ask, I don't think I have a choice but to say yes," I told him with tears in my eyes.

"Oh, you do have a choice, but you better choose right so I won't kill your little ass."

Everybody started laughing as we kissed, and then Reeno stood to congratulate his brother while Eden stood to congratulate me.

"Oh my god! Let me see that ring, girl." Eden grabbed my hand to examine the ring that was just placed on my finger. This is one of the best nights of my life.

Chapter 27

Eden

Six Months Later

Some would say that Reeno and I fell in love too quickly, but who are they to judge? Love had no time frame. I loved that man with all of me. Yes, we started off on the wrong foot with bullets flying past my head and hoes trying to claim what was mine, but it was all good. Nothing could break our bond, and that has been proven so far.

I sat on the edge of the bed in our new home, waiting on Reeno to bring my shoes to me and put them on.   The night that Raydon proposed to Destiny, I had my own surprise. I was three months pregnant, and after things settled from the astonishment of Raydon asking Destiny to marry him, I let the cat out the bag.

Reeno was thrilled to know that I was carrying his baby. His ass said that this baby meant that we were going to be together forever. That same night, he told me to look for a house, and I did. We lived in the same neighborhood as Raydon and Destiny, but about a mile down the road.

My water broke ten minutes ago, and Reeno was running from room to room, getting on my mothafuckin' nerves like we hadn't went over this shit numerous times. It's like everything went out of the window. All I needed were my shoes and the hospital bag. Here I am in labor, and this masculine ass man is acting like a punk. I can't wait to rub this in his face. It would be comical if these contractions weren't kicking my ass.

"Reeno! shouted, grabbing his attention.

He stopped, turning toward me with his eyebrow raised, not saying anything.

"Calm down, babe. We've been over this. I need my shoes, and my hospital bag is in the closet."

He sighed as he bent down to pick up my shoes and then walked over to put them on my feet. He then stared into my eyes and spoke. "My bad, baby. A nigga just excited as fuck." He stood and kissed me before walking to the closet and getting my hospital bag. It was go time.

"I know you are. I am too. Now let's go. Ahhhhhhh!"

I grabbed Reeno's arm and squeezed the hell out of it until my contraction passed.

"Shit, woman," left his lips when I finally let go.

He then slipped his phone into his pocket before scooping me up bridal style, carrying me down the steps and into the garage. He used my key fob to unlock the door to my truck.

"We're taking my car?" I asked, confused because he never drove my truck.

"Hell yeah. You not gettin' that shit in my car," he exclaimed with a straight face.

I just left it alone because he was serious. I guess he didn't realize that either way, he was going to be cleaning a car out.

I was finally situated in the front seat as comfortable as I could be. Reeno moved to the driver's seat after placing my seat belt on the best he could over my big ass belly. He pressed the garage door opener, which was above my sun visor, and backed out en route to Carolinas Medical Center Matthews.

"Babe, call Destiny." I waited as he connected his phone to my car and dialed her number.

"Hello," she answered lazily since it was two in the morning.

"Aye, Des, get to the hospital. Her water broke." Reeno spoke with urgency.

"Destiny, this shit hurts!" I screamed.

"Awww, babe. We on the way."

Reeno hung up and grabbed my hand, lacing our fingers together before saying, "You got this, baby. You strong as shit, and this is no different from anything else that you do."

******

"Push, Eden, push. You got this, baby girl." Reeno was beside me, holding my hand, telling me to push as the doctor sat at my feet, coaching me on when to push.

Sweat trickled down my body as I struggled to push our son out. Giving birth was one of the hardest, yet one of the most beautiful things I had to do. I turned my head to look at Reeno with tears running down my cheeks and to grab some of his strength. Finally, after ten hours of labor, and thirty minutes pushing him out, our son, Reeno Brooks Jr. was born.

It took a minute for my eyes to open and realize that I wasn't the only one in the room.

"She's up?" I heard Destiny ask. I looked around and also saw Raydon, and Mr. and Mrs. Brooks.

I smiled at her and asked, "Where is he?"

"We're right here."

Reeno came into view with a tiny being in his arms. He stood beside the bed, placing our son in my arms, followed by kissing me gently on the lips. I looked down at my son, beaming at how he was a perfect mixture of his father and me. His curly hair was so soft I could touch it all day. His cute little button nose and tiny little body, I was so in love.

"He looks like the both of you." Mrs. Brooks beamed.

"You did good, son." Mr. Brooks patted Reeno on his shoulder.

"Yeah, we did that shit, babe." Reeno held out his hand for a high-five. I shook my head as I high-fived his ass.

"I told you that you were going to be mine forever, and I meant that shit."

Reeno had a grin on his face, along with everyone else. Not paying too much attention to him, I watched as my son held my finger, making baby noises and flailing his legs. The view was so cute. When I finally looked up, Reeno was holding a box with a big ass diamond in it.

"Baby, you fuckin' with me forever or what?"

When I tell you everyone in that room burst into laughter… This man of mine was a fool, but I loved his non-romantic ass.

"Yes, baby. I'm fuckin' with you forever."

I held on to my baby tight as he placed the ring on my finger. He leaned forward, kissing me before kissing our son on his forehead. I remember at some point I wasn't sure if I wanted a life with someone of his caliber, but after being with him, I wouldn't trade him for the world.

The End

Note from Author

I hope you all enjoyed this story. I know I enjoyed writing it. I love all of my readers and it's because of you guys that I continue to write these stories,

I love keeping in touch with my readers. You guys are awesome!

Facebook
Facebook.com/quishasreaders

Instagram
Quisha_dynae

Twitter
@quishadynae

E-mail
Quishadynae@yahoo.com

Also check out the website to the annual Queen City Book Fair at Qcbookfair.com.

Other books by Quisha Dynae

-Bad Boys Ain't no Good: Good Boys Ain't no Fun 1-2

-Not Gon' Cry

-Love the Way You Lie

-Love the Way you Lie, too

-Side Nigga

-Your Love Belongs to me 1-2

-Sydney Valentine: Craving Love

-Yancey and Ariel: Loving Him Through it all 1-2

-Lick of a Lifetime

-Seasons of Love: Summer's Story

-Seasons of Love: Autumn's Story

-Seasons of Love: Wynter's Story

Made in the USA
Columbia, SC
16 December 2018